SHOWDOWN TRAIL

LESLIE SCOTT

THORNDIKE
CHIVERS

This Large Print edition is published by Thorndike Press, Waterville, Maine, USA and by AudioGO Ltd, Bath, England.

Thorndike Press, a part of Gale, Cengage Learning.

LIBRARY OF CONGRESS CATALOGING-IN-PUBLICATION DATA

Scott, Leslie, 1893–1975.
    Showdown trail / by Leslie Scott. — Large print ed.
      p. cm. — (Thorndike Press large print western)
    ISBN-13: 978-1-4104-4099-0 (hardcover)
    ISBN-10: 1-4104-4099-0 (hardcover)
    1. Large type books. I. Title.
  PS3537.C9265.S56 2011
  813'.54—dc22   2011021730

BRITISH LIBRARY CATALOGUING-IN-PUBLICATION DATA AVAILABLE

Published in 2011 in the U.S. by arrangement with Golden West Literary Agency.

Published in 2012 in the U.K. by arrangement with Golden West Literary Agency.

U.K. Hardcover: 978 1 445 86053 4 (Chivers Large Print)
U.K. Softcover: 978 1 445 86054 1 (Camden Large Print)

Printed and bound in Great Britain by the MPG Books Group
1 2 3 4 5 6 7 15 14 13 12 11

C

SHOWDOWN TRAIL

SHOWDOWN TRAIL

CHAPTER I

Shimmering whitely in the blaze of the Texas sunlight, the Tornaga Trail flowed along the base of a range of jagged hills. The outstretching branches of encroaching growth threw bars of blue-black across the dusty surface. The wind raised the dust in little spurts and puffs or whirled it in a weird devil-dance, the spinning particles glinting silver in the clear air. Beyond the belt of growth rolled the rangeland, purple-green tipped with the amethyst of the seeding grass heads. To the south, still miles distant, surged the yellow flood of the Rio Grande, with the many-coloured mountains of Mexico beyond. And less than three miles distant was the only pass through the Tornaga Hills, which in a less lofty terrain would have been dignified as mountains.

The trail was silent with the soft-edged 'silence' of late summer. Only the slight wind rustling of the stiff growth and the drowsy buzz of the cicadas disturbed the overall blanket of stillness. The Tornaga was a torpid snake with nowhere to go.

Gradually an alien sound cut through the thin undertone of small noises.

Around the bend to the north bulged a dozen riders, grim-faced, alert men who peered ahead with hard, watchful eyes and urged their foam-flecked horses to greater speed.

'Boys, we're gaining on them,' old Arch Carol, owner of the Luck Seven Ranch, jolted out in rhythm to the strides of his big roan.

'We are,' replied Jim Weston, his range boss, 'but if we don't catch them before they get through the Pass, we're done. One man with a rifle at the other end of that crack could hold off fifty.'

'The nerve of those sidewinders, running off a herd in broad daylight!' Carol said in a jerky growl.

'And if they'd killed Gus Hawkins, like they thought they did, instead of just creasing him, they'd have gotten away with it, because we wouldn't have learned of it in time to run them down,' answered Weston. 'As it is, we've got our work cut out for us.'

'How the devil did the hellions know those cows were being held in that canyon?' Carol wanted to know.

'I can't say,' replied Weston. 'The important thing isn't how they knew, but the fact that they did know, just as it seems owlhoots know everything that goes on in this section. Sift sand! We've no time to lose.'

The troop surged on, the horses labouring on the steep grade, leaning far over as they swerved around a bend. Suddenly the hills reeled back as if smashed by a giant fist, and the pass, a suspension bridge swinging in the sky, lunged into view. The northern mouth was wide, but to the south it narrowed to a mere crack through which the cattle would shoot like pips squeezed from an orange. The gorge was swathed in a blue mist, with a shifting of colour from delicate azure to a whitish yellow where a dust cloud rolled up.

'There they are, the murderin' thieves, and they ain't made the pass yet!' yelled big Tom Peters. 'After 'em, boys; we've got 'em!'

It looked that way, but Jim Weston knew the rustlers weren't caught yet, not by a jugful. There were more than a dozen of them, and they were hard men; wide-loopers in the Texas Big Bend country were seldom gentle lambs. They were urging the stolen herd forward at top speed, making for the shelter of the pass and the sanctuary beyond that was the Rio Grande and Mexico.

'Get set,' Weston told his men as they closed the distance. 'This isn't going to be any Sunday school picnic.'

The wide-loopers were glancing back over their shoulders at the pursuit, gauging the distance. Men riding point and flank along the strung-out herd began falling back, leaving only three or four riders to urge the cattle into the pass. The others strung out in the rear of the herd.

'Hunker down in your hulls,' shouted Weston. 'We'll have some blue whistlers around our ears in a minute.'

In the wide-flung jaws of the pass, the fight opened. From the ranks of the outlaws came puffs of smoke, followed by the lethal whine of passing lead and the crackle of rifles.

'Hold your fire,' cautioned Weston. 'Ride!'

The Lucky Seven punchers rode, sweeping forward in open-rank formation, waiting for Weston to give the word. The outlaw rifles continued to crack, but the distance was too great for anything like accurate shooting. Weston counted off the wide-loopers' dwindling lead — six hundred yards, five-fifty, five hundred, four-fifty. His voice rang out:

'Let them have it!'

Rifles leaped to shoulders; the muzzles spurted orange flame. Three saddles were emptied. But the outlaws fought back grimly. A Lucky Seven cowboy cursed shrilly as a bullet tore through the flesh of his upper arm and nearly hurled him from the saddle. He grabbed the horn, recovered, straightened, and fired his rifle with one hand. At the same instant another hand gave a queer little coughing grunt and slewed sideways to the ground.

Weston, well in front, fired with steady aim. He saw a rustler fling up his hands and fall. Another rose in his stirrups, lurched forward and went down like a dropped sack of old clothes. His companions' guns were blazing and their yells quivered in his eardrums.

Now only two of the wide-loopers' rearguard remained, and they had had enough of it. They whirled their horses, went racing along the side of the bellowing herd. Those urging the cattle on glanced back, faced to the front and rode for their lives. The Lucky Seven hands whooped with triumph and drummed in pursuit.

But their horses were already blowing and exhausted. Besides, the gorge was narrowing, and they had to force their way through the straggle of the herd. Weston's voice rang out.

'Hold it!' he shouted. 'Turn the cows and start them to milling. We can't catch what's left of them. Didn't do so bad as it is. Is Short badly hurt?'

Before he got an answer, big Tom Peters foamed his horse in alongside the range boss. His face was haggard, his eyes wild.

'My God, Jim, the Old Man got it!' he croaked hoarsely. 'Come along; he's asking for you. Hurry; he won't last long.'

Weston whirled his horse and rode back to where Arch Carol lay on the ground, his men grouped around him. Weston flung himself from the saddle with his horse still in motion and knelt beside the owner. Carol gazed up into his face with eyes that were already becoming fixed. Weston glanced at his bared chest. Just below the heart and a little to the right was a small blue hole, with a frothing bubble of blood rising and falling at its edges. Weston's face set like granite. He knew all too well what that frothy bubble meant.

Arch Carol spoke, his voice a reedy whisper. 'Can't do anything, Jim — I'm filling up inside — cut something big — listen — my sister Leah gets the spread — lawyer Jarret has papers — knows where she is — Chicago — all kin folks I got — she'll sell

— don't know nothing about running spread — see she gets fair price — depending on you, Jim — look — after — Leah — good — kid ——'

The whisper trailed off. Carol's eyes closed wearily. His chest arched as he fought for air. It fell in, and did not rise again. Jim Weston bowed his head, slipped a clean handkerchief from his pocket and reverently laid it over the Old Man's dead face. He stood up. His pale eyes were terrible, but his voice was quiet when he said:

'Tie him and Short to their saddles. Then turn those cows, and back to the spread.'

Tom Peters shook his fist toward the south and rumbled profanity.

'Swearing won't help,' Weston said. 'Come on; we've got work to do.'

They buried Arch Carol and Earl Short under the whispering pines on the hill above the Lucky Seven ranch-house. The funeral was attended by all the section's cowmen, including tall, handsome Nelson Haynes, owner of the big Bar H, whose condolences Jim Weston received in silence.

Weston put in a busy week straightening out matters pertaining to the ranch. Then he rode to Marta to consult with Lawyer Floyd Jarrett.

'I wrote to Arch's sister, Miss Leah Carol,

13

who is working in Chicago, as soon as I was notified of his death,' said the lawyer. 'I explained to her what had happened and the terms of the will, which I have in my safe. She inherits everything without reservation, to dispose of as she sees fit.'

'I suppose she'll sell?' suggested Weston.

'It's logical to believe so,' agreed Jarrett. 'She'd hardly take over running the spread herself, knowing nothing of the cattle business.'

Weston was silent a moment; then:

'Floyd, I'd like to buy the Lucky Seven,' he said. 'I can't offer what the spread's worth as a property, but I have a few pesos salted away, and I can offer what, in this section, would be considered a fair purchase price.'

'Jim, there's nothing I'd like better to see happen,' said Jarrett, 'but I'm afraid Nelson Haynes will outbid you. I happen to know he is eager to acquire the property to round out his holdings.'

'Floyd, Arch Carol would never have sold to Haynes,' Weston said. 'You know that as well as I do. When Haynes approached him nearly two years back, he refused to consider his proposition and was mighty short about it.'

'Yes, I know,' nodded the lawyer.

'No, he wouldn't sell to Haynes,' Weston repeated. 'And Haynes made him what was, conditions being what they were at the time, a very attractive offer. I asked him why he wouldn't take Haynes up on it, and he said he'd tell me why later. Never did, though. Guess he never got around to it, and I never asked again. He had some reason for not wanting to sell to Haynes, but what it was I don't know.'

'I don't either,' replied Jarrett, 'but whatever it was, it doesn't count for anything now, with poor Arch out of the picture. Arch didn't like Nelson Haynes, though for no particular reason, so far as I could learn. Haynes, however, is a comparative newcomer to this section, with progressive ideas. I'm forced to admit he's a bit arrogant and impatient with what he considers outmoded methods. He's rubbed quite a few old-timers the wrong way, including Arch Carol.'

'Carol never would have sold to him,' Weston repeated.

'Admittedly so,' answered the lawyer, 'but I have an obligation to my client and must make the best deal possible for her. After all, the matter won't be in my hands; she must make her own decisions. I can only advise what I think best for her interests. I received a reply to my letter today. She has decided to come out from Chicago and look things over for herself.'

'The devil she has!' exclaimed Weston. 'A long trip for an old lady. I imagine she's just about poor Arch's age, one way or another, and he was pushing sixty.'

'I imagine so,' said Jarrett. 'Can't say as Arch ever mentioned how old she was. Only spoke of her when he commissioned me to draw up his will.'

'I recall him mentioning a sister back East once or twice, but that's about all,' replied Weston. 'Arch never was much of a talker. And so she's coming to look things over?'

'Yes. Will arrive on the noon train Friday, she wrote,' said Jarrett. 'You'd better meet her with a buckboard, Jim. I presume she'd find a twenty-mile ride on horseback a bit rough.'

'If she could manage to back a horse,' grunted Weston. 'Okay, I'll be here Friday at noon, with cushions and blankets.'

Floyd Jarrett chuckled as Weston headed for the door.

CHAPTER II

The two girls sat on the edge of the bed in their nightgowns and talked. Leah Carol was small and slender, with wide blue eyes and a mop of curly red-brown hair. Rose Erwin, her room-mate, was buxom, cheerful and almost always smiling.

But Rose wasn't smiling at the moment. She was serious and looked decidedly perturbed.

'Leah, you're not really going, are you?' she asked for at least the tenth time.

'Yes, Rose, I am,' the red-haired girl replied in tones of finality. She glanced toward the window outside which Chicago roared and bustled, although the hour was late. 'I'm not made for the city, Rose. Remember, I was brought up on a farm. But the farm was worn out and mortgaged, and when Dad and Mother died there was nothing left for me. So I had to come to the city and get a job. But I don't like it and it's

17

not good for me.'

She stood up abruptly and crossed to the cheap dresser, on which lay an open letter. She picked up the letter and studied it, a little wrinkle showing between her dark brows.

Rose studied Leah. No, the city wasn't good for Leah, she was forced to admit. A year before, when Leah had come into the office and the two girls had decided to share a room to cut down expenses, she had been different. Then there had been colour in her softly rounded cheeks and she had had curves where curves belonged. Now her cheeks were pale and slightly hollow, and there was a pinched look about her sweetly formed mouth.

Poor kid's almost skinny, Rose mused. She ought to eat more.

But Rose knew well it was not lack of food that was pulling Leah down. Yes, Leah was right: the city did not agree with her.

'But way off in Texas,' Rose voiced a last protest, 'where there's nothing but wild cowboys and Indians and rattlesnakes and deserts and goodness knows what else!'

Leah turned with a smile. 'Oh, I don't think it's so bad as all that,' she replied. 'Of course I don't know much about it myself, except what I gathered from the letters brother Arch wrote and what he told us when he visited us years ago. But from what he said and wrote, it's a pretty nice country, once you get used to it. He said it was beautiful, with mountains and streams and miles and miles of land where the grass grows almost as high as my head.'

'That wouldn't be so very high,' Rose interpolated, 'but go on.'

'Arch wrote he had thousands of cows on his ranch,' Leah continued.

'Thousands of cows!' Rose wailed. 'How in the world could you milk thousands of cows?'

'Silly,' Leah laughed, 'you don't milk them. They call all kinds of cattle cows out there. You sell them for beef.'

'You mean you have to butcher them?' Rose gasped. 'You'll get your hands all bloody!'

Leah laughed again. 'The owner of the cows doesn't butcher them,' she explained. 'He ships them to the packing houses in Kansas City or Omaha or right here in Chicago. They're butchered at the packing houses.'

'Well, that doesn't sound quite so bad,' Rose admitted doubtfully.

Leah was still studying the letter. 'There's a lot of legal language here I don't perfectly understand,' she said, 'but I do understand that I am Arch's sole heir.' She continued reminiscently, almost to herself, 'Arch Carol was not really my brother, but my half-brother. Dad married a second time, late in life, after his first wife had been dead for many years, and I was the result. I only saw Arch once, when I was a little girl and he came to visit us. I liked him, and he seemed to take to me right off. Wrote me many times after he went back to Texas. He was old when he visited us, or at least he seemed old to me, although I guess he really wasn't much more than forty. After Dad died, and Mother just a year later, he wanted me to come and live with him. But Texas seemed an awful long way off. Besides, I didn't want to be dependent on him. I guess I inherited that streak from Dad, who was very independent. He never let Arch know that things weren't going so good for him in his old age. And I thought I could make out all right in Chicago. The lawyer writes that he has a purchaser for the property, if I don't care to come out and run it.'

'I think you'd better take the money and forget all about the ranch,' advised Rose. 'You could buy a farm with it here close to Chicago, and I could come and visit you at vacation time.'

'I'll expect you to come and visit me anyhow,' Leah replied. 'You might marry a handsome cowboy.'

'And live in a bunkhouse,' Rose sniffed. 'I've heard that's what they call the place where cowboys live.'

'You might find it interesting and exciting,' Leah dimpled.

'I'm going,' she concluded. 'I've already given notice at the office and wired the lawyer when to expect me.'

Leah packed her bags, said a tearful farewell to Rose and shook the dust of Chicago off her high heels, hoping never to see the Windy City again.

Before the long train ride came to an end, Leah Carol was heartily weary of it. One morning she awakened to see what seemed utterly endless miles of grass-grown land flowing past the Pullman window.

'Aren't we ever going to reach Texas?' she despairingly asked the waiter in the dining car as he served her breakfast.

'Why, ma'am,' chuckled the waiter, his genial black countenance all one great grin, 'we been passing through Texas for the last ten hours.'

'Ten hours!' Leah gasped, glancing out the window at the telegraph poles whisking past like the pickets of a fence.

'Yessum,' replied the waiter. 'You're going to Marta, I believe you said. Be another three hours 'fore we get there, and then you'll still be in Texas. It's a pow'ful big state.'

'Why, you could travel from Chicago to New York in that time,' she said.

'Yessum,' agreed the waiter, 'and if you laid Texas down up there you'd just about be travelling all the way on Texas from Chicago to New York. It's a big state, ma'am.'

Before Leah finished her breakfast she realised that the country was changing. Distant ranges of mountains cut the skyline. The train crossed patches of desert. The mountains and the hills edged closer. She glimpsed cactus, gnarled and twisted little trees, tall stalks that shot twenty or thirty feet into the air to explode in starry white blossoms. She thrilled to the beauty of this wild and alien land.

Marta, on the northern edge of the Texas Big Bend country, proved to be a treeless little town, its board sidewalks lined with shacks and false fronts. The dust of its wide main street shimmered with heat. Everywhere Leah looked she could see mountains fanging into the intense blue of the sky, with wide stretches of rolling grassland between the ranges.

As she was staring about helplessly, the doors of a saloon across the street from the railroad station swung open. A tall and very broad-shouldered man on whose lean face was a stubble of black beard came out, wiping his mouth with the back of his hand. He wore overalls, a faded blue shirt, high-heeled scuffed boots and a broad-brimmed grey hat. Leah's eyes widened a little as she noticed that around his lean waist were two crossed belts with leather loops sewed to them. The loops were studded with gleaming brass cartridges. At either hip swung a black gun that looked enormous to Leah. As he strode lithely across the street, glancing inquiringly about, a perplexed expression on his face, and mounted the board sidewalk, he seemed a veritable giant to the small girl, although really he was but a little more than six feet in height.

Leah experienced a feeling of near-panic as he walked straight toward her, regarding her with a pair of rather long eyes that appeared startlingly pale in his dark face. When he reached her, he paused and removed the big hat, revealing thick, crisp hair so black a blue shadow seemed to lie upon it.

'Pardon me, ma'am,' he said in a deep but

23

musical voice, 'you got off the train, didn't you?'

'Yes,' Leah managed to reply.

'And,' he said, 'did you by any chance see an old biddy get off maybe at the last station?'

'Why, no,' Leah answered. 'I think only a couple of men got off at the station before this one, and nobody at the station before that.'

The big man glanced around. 'Now where in blazes did she get to?' he wondered in exasperated tones. 'She was supposed to get here on the noon train, and I was supposed to meet her here. Blast it! You can never depend on a woman doing the right thing. I suppose she missed the train, and never thought to notify Jarrett or me that she'd be in on another one,' he added as if talking to himself.

Leah caught the name 'Jarrett', and it struck a responsive chord in her memory. She glanced up at her interrogator.

'Do you happen to know the lady's name?' she asked.

'Carol,' he grunted. 'Miss Leah Carol. Yes, I suppose she missed the train.'

'No, she didn't miss the train,' Leah said.

The pale grey eyes shot her a quick glance. 'What do you mean, ma'am?' he asked.

'I mean that she arrived here on the noon train,' Leah replied. 'I happen to be Miss Leah Carol, the old biddy you were supposed to meet.'

The tall man's lean jaw sagged. He stared at her. 'But — but,' he stammered, 'she was supposed to be an old lady.'

'Give her time and she will be,' Leah answered, feeling sorry for his confusion. 'Do you mind telling me who you are?'

'I'm Jim Weston, the Lucky Seven range boss,' he replied, recovering somewhat from his bewilderment. 'I was to meet you here and drive you out to the ranch-house. First, though, Lawyer Jarrett down the street would like to see you. He asked me to bring you to his office as soon as you got in.'

'Well, I'm ready,' Leah replied. 'Yes, these are my bags.'

He picked them up with one hand, apparently paying no heed to their weight.

'Right down the street,' he repeated, and strode off, evidently expecting her to follow.

Leah caught up with him in a few quick steps. He did not glance at her. Apparently once he had corralled her, she ceased to exist as far as he was concerned.

A little way down the street Weston paused before one of the false-fronts, pushed open a door and stood aside to let her enter first.

25

Leah found herself in a small room lined with bookshelves. Seated at a table was a genial-looking old man with twinkling brown eyes. Leah felt at home with him at once.

'Hello, Jim,' he greeted Weston. His glance included Leah. 'And what can I do for you, young lady?'

'Floyd, this is her,' Weston said ungrammatically.

'Her?'

'Miss Leah Carol, Arch Carol's sister.'

The lawyer's astonishment was equal to that evinced by Weston shortly before, but he quickly recovered his aplomb.

'Well, well!' he chuckled. 'This *is* a surprise. I had expected somebody older.' His shrewd eyes looked Leah up and down.

'Jim,' he said, 'I'm darned if she doesn't look like Arch, doesn't she? Arch had the same colour red hair before it got grey. She's got the same shape nose, too, only smaller. And darned if there aren't a couple of freckles on it just like Arch had on his. Same chin, too, except hers is round and Arch's was square. But she don't look over pert. Arch was a husky jigger. Come to think of it, though, when he showed up here, near thirty years back, he was sort of ganglin'. Texas air does things for folks, ma'am. Look at Jim there. If he'd been born back East the chances are he wouldn't have been knee-high to a horned toad.'

Leah laughed outright. Lawyer Floyd Jarrett was refreshing. Jim Weston's reaction to the harangue was a grunt.

'You need a shave, Jim,' chattered the lawyer, scratching about amid the papers that littered the table.

'I've had work to do,' Weston replied in surly tones.

'Of course, of course,' agreed Jarrett. 'Now, Leah, here are a few papers for you to look over and sign, and then this business will be all cleared up. As I wrote you, I have a purchaser for the property who will give you a fair price.'

'I brought bank and business references with me and a letter of identification, along with the letter you wrote me,' Leah said, glancing at the papers and refraining from comment on the lawyer's last statement.

'You can leave 'em with me and I'll look 'em over when I get time,' said Jarrett. 'Guess you don't need any identification to anybody who knew Arch Carol; you're the spittin' image of him, in a lot prettier way, don't you think so, Jim?'

From Mr. Weston, another grunt.

'Now put you name right here, Leah, and

here, and here,' Jarrett continued. 'Okay, that does it. She's your boss now, Jim, and will hand out the powders.'

Grunt number three from Mr. Weston.

Leah shot him a somewhat puzzled glance. It seemed to her that his eyes were distinctly hostile as they rested on her. She wondered why, or if she could be mistaken.

'Take her out and get her something to eat before you leave town, Jim,' Jarrett advised. 'Drop in when you're ready to talk business relative to the sale of the ranch, Leah. Jim can line you up on anything you want to know, and you can depend on what he says.'

'I'll be seeing you soon, Mr. Jarrett,' Leah promised, not committing herself further. 'It's a pleasure to know you.'

The old lawyer beamed. Weston, in silence, picked up the bags again and led the way from the office. A few doors along the street, he turned in.

Leah was slightly startled when she realised that the restaurant was also a saloon. Spurred and booted men lined the bar, most of them packing guns. They shot swift glances in her direction as she entered, then appeared to forget all about her, although in reality they were studying her in the back-bar mirror and she was the chief topic of their low-voiced conversation.

'Slab of cow all right?' Weston asked as they sat down.

Leah suddenly realised that she was ravenously hungry, hungrier than she could remember being for a year. Maybe there was something to what Lawyer Jarrett had said about Texas air.

'I suppose you mean a steak,' she replied. 'That will be fine.'

When the steak appeared, it was a slab all right, but it was tender and deliciously cooked. To her surprise, Leah finished it to the last bite, along with bread and butter and a liberal portion of fried potatoes.

As they ate in silence, she covertly studied Jim Weston. She noted that his slender, powerful-looking hands manipulated his knife and fork correctly and with unconscious ease.

'Eats like a gentleman, even though he doesn't act like one,' she told herself. 'Range boss. I seem to remember Arch mentioning that corresponds to a foreman back home. I don't think he's glad to see me here, for some reason or other. Well, I guess it doesn't matter.'

As soon as they finished eating, Weston led the way outside. 'Got a long ride ahead of us,' he explained. 'You wait here in the shade while I get the team. Be right back.'

He strode up the street, taking her bags with him. Leah watched him turn a corner.

In a surprisingly short time he came back around the corner, on the high seat of a buckboard drawn by four dancing horses. Weston pulled them to a slithering halt.

'Climb up,' he called. 'I can't let go these jugheads to help you.'

Leah climbed to the high seat, giving various interested onlookers a view of a very shapely leg and ankle. The horses shot forward, and the buckboard roared out of town in a cloud of dust. Leah jammed her perky little hat down on her red curls and held on for dear life. She caught the flicker of a derisive glance from the corners of Jim Weston's pale eyes. Her red lips set firmly. A moment later she leaned forward and peered over the dash-board.

'The breeching strap on the off-wheeler is too tight,' she said.

Weston's head jerked around. 'What's that?' he exclaimed.

'I said the breeching strap on the off-wheeler is too tight,' Leah repeated. 'It's cramping his stride. When we start up the hill over there, I'll hold the team while you loosen it a notch. I was brought up on a farm, Mr. Weston, and I know horses and how they should be harnessed.'

Weston stared at her for an instant. 'Okay,' was all he said. When they reached the steep grade of the opposite sag, he pulled the team to a halt. Leah held them while he remedied the offending strap. He climbed back to the seat without a word.

All the long afternoon the buckboard rolled south-by-west, seldom slackening speed. Leah thrilled to the wild beauty of the desolate land and was so absorbed in the constantly varying scenery that she paid scant heed to Weston's taciturnity. She felt this was no place for small talk. Silence was preferable.

Jim suddenly turned to the girl beside him on the seat.

'Pardon, ma'am,' he said, 'but do you aim to spend any time here before disposing of the ranch?'

Leah glanced up at him, and her lips tightened. 'Mr. Weston,' she replied, 'I am here to stay, definitely. I know I am going to love this country. Yes, I hope to spend quite a lot of time here, if I'm spared that long. I have no intention of selling the ranch. I am going to stay here and operate the property.'

Weston's eyes widened with incredulous disbelief. 'You don't mean it?' he spluttered.

'I mean exactly what I said,' Leah answered.

Gazing at her, Weston suddenly realised that there *was* a startling resemblance to Arch Carol. When Arch had set his mind on something, nothing could change him.

Leah bit her lip to stifle a laugh. His dismay was really ludicrous.

'Oh, I realise that I know nothing about ranching,' she said. 'But I intend to learn, and I think you will be able to help me, despite your grumpiness.'

'Grumpiness!' he exploded.

'Yes. I think that is just the word for it. You appear to be going out of your way to be disagreeable to me. But we will let that pass. I gather that you have the interests of the Lucky Seven at heart, and I don't believe you will let personal dislike stand in the way of those interests. Yes, grumpiness is the right word. In fact, you remind me of an old shorthorn bull we had on the farm back in Illinois. He was always grunting and growling and glowering. Inside, however, he was really a gentle and affectionate beast, and liked to have his ears scratched and his head rubbed.'

Jim Weston drew a deep breath. Somehow he was reminded of how he had felt once in the fourth grade when his teacher had caught him putting a live frog in her desk drawer and told him off for fair.

'Yes, I do have the interests of the Lucky Seven at heart,' he said, and let it go at that. Leah nodded, and gazed straight ahead. There was no further conversation between them.

The lovely blue dusk had sifted down from the hilltops, and it was almost full dark when they pulled into the yard of a small but tightly built ranch-house set in a grove of burr oaks. Leah caught a glimpse of what she decided must be the bunk-house, a large barn and other buildings. Weston let out a shout, and a man in overalls came running to take charge of the team. He slipped to the ground, reached up and lifted Leah down as if she were a feather. Picking up her bags, he led the way up the steps and across the wide veranda.

In the doorway stood a little gnome of a man not a bit bigger than Leah herself. His face was a multitude of wrinkles, his hair snow white and his black eyes as bright as polished buttons. His faded shirt and overalls were spotless. Altogether, Leah thought he was the cleanest-looking man she had ever laid eyes on, and the kindliest. His warm grin instantly dissipated the loneliness which had begun to gather about her heart.

'This is Dirty-Shirt Jones, the cook,' Weston announced. 'Dirty, this is Miss Carol, the new owner. Look after her.'

'Come in! Come in!' squeaked Dirty-Shirt. 'I'll take you up to the room I reckon you'll want to use, and show you where everything is.'

He grabbed the bags from Weston and led her into the house, smiling and chuckling. Leah found herself in a big, comfortably furnished room with a fireplace and a beamed ceiling. At the far end were stairs which Dirty-Shirt mounted. Leah followed him, leaving Weston standing in the doorway.

Dirty-Shirt flung open a door at the head of the stairs. 'Here you are,' he squeaked. 'This is the one Arch had. Jim has always slept in the one across the hall. I sleep in the back. Reckon you'll want us to move to the bunk-house, though.'

'I certainly will not,' Leah told him with emphasis. 'Why should I? Do you think I want to sleep in this big house all alone?'

Dirty-Shirt grinned and chuckled. 'I dunno,' he replied. 'Wimmen folks is apt to be finicky. That's been my experience.'

'Well,' Leah smiled as she removed her hat and tossed it on the wide and comfortable-looking bed. 'I think you need some more experience. You'll find I'm not.'

Dirty-Shirt gurgled delightedly. 'Chuck will be on the table for you and Jim as soon as you come down,' he said. 'The boys has already et.'

Astonishingly hungry again, Leah enjoyed an excellent dinner, while old Dirty-Shirt pattered about benignly, supplying her needs. Weston ate in silence and rose to his feet as soon as he finished.

'See you in the morning, ma'am,' he said, and left the ranch-house.

'What in the world is the matter with him?' Leah demanded of Dirty-Shirt. 'He acts as if he didn't have a bit of use for me and resents me being here.'

Dirty-Shirt countered with a question of his own. 'You going to sell out, ma'am?'

'I am not,' Leah told him emphatically. 'I'm going to live here and run the ranch.'

Dirty-Shirt nodded his white head. 'I sort of gathered you were going to do just that,' he said. 'Uh-huh, I sort of figured it. Well, for one thing, cowhands don't usually take over well to working for a lady boss. Superstitious horned toads and think it's bad luck. And Jim is kinda put out, anyhow. He'd hoped to maybe buy out your brother some day, when Arch got a bit older and decided to take it easy. Your brother passing on sort of scrambled things.'

'I see,' Leah replied. So Weston was the prospective buyer the lawyer had mentioned. That angle required some thought. Quite likely Weston figured she would eventually get tired of responsibility and decide to sell. Well, he was in for a disappointment.

'But Jim's a fine feller,' Dirty-Shirt hastened to add. 'He can shoot a fly off the end of a sixty-foot rope and not graze a fibre, and I reckon he can whip any two men in Texas.'

'Outstanding qualifications,' Leah remarked with a sarcasm that was lost on Dirty-Shirt.

'He knows the cow business, too,' resumed the old cook, 'up and down both sides and through the middle. He just about run the spread for the past two years, after Arch Carol got to having attacks of the miseries that laid him up a good part of the time. Backin' a horse ain't good for any kind of rheumatism.'

'I see,' Leah repeated. 'Now I think I'll go to bed — I'm utterly tired out. I don't sleep well on trains.'

'If you happen to want anything durin' the night, I'm in the back,' said Dirty-Shirt. 'And Jim's right across the hall.'

'Thank you. I'll come to the back if I want anything,' Leah answered. Dirty-Shirt chuckled and began removing the dishes.

In the bunk-house, Jim Weston faced the assembled Lucky Seven punchers.

'Well, she's here,' he said. 'A skinny little wench, all eyes, with red hair.'

'Dyed, I reckon,' snorted cantankerous old Sam Hardy. 'Arch's was grey, mighty nigh white.'

'No, it isn't dyed,' Weston differed.

'No? How old is she, anyhow?'

'About twenty-one or two, but looks younger,' Weston replied.

The cowboys stared.

'But — how — what — how come?' sputtered Tom Peters. 'Arch was nigh on to sixty. You sure she's his sister, Jim?'

'One look at her when she gets her dander up is enough to tell you,' said Weston. 'Then she's Arch Carol all over when he was set to land on somebody with all four feet.'

Peters shook his head in bewilderment. 'How come she got her dander up?' he asked irrelevantly.

'Never mind,' Weston answered. 'She did.'

'Well, reckon Nelson Haynes will be taking over soon,' sighed Peters. 'Wonder if the H Open A H is hiring?' Despondent mutters ran through the bunk-house.

Jim Weston dropped his bombshell.

'She's not going to sell to Haynes. She's going to stay here and run the spread herself.'

His hearers stared at him in slack-jawed amazement.

'Going to run it herself!' howled Sam Hardy. 'How in blazes can a twenty-year-old brat run a cow factory?'

'And I sure don't hanker to work for a woman,' growled Peters. 'I'm going to ask for my time.'

'You won't get it,' Weston told him flatly. 'And that goes for the rest of you. I promised Arch Carol to look after her interests, and that's just what I aim to do. You're all staying on, and so am I, till she gets the hang of things. Anybody who feels like arguing the point, I'll try to accommodate.'

There were no takers. 'Arguing' with Jim Weston had been tried once or twice, with small enjoyment for the arguer.

'Oh, well, maybe things won't be too bad,' observed the optimistic Peters. 'Jim will run the spread, and she'll just tag along.'

'Maybe,' said Weston. 'Somehow she didn't strike me as the tagging-along sort. Anyhow, that's the way the situation stands and we'll have to make the best of it.'

The Lucky Seven hands agreed, and

proceeded to drown their sorrows in a couple of poker games that lasted until far into the night.

CHAPTER III

Leah slept dreamlessly. She didn't even hear Jim Weston come in, pause a moment at the head of the stairs, and then enter his own room across the hall. When she descended to the dining-room the cowboys were just coming in for breakfast. She took her place at the head of the table and the meal proceeded in decorous silence.

Leah stood it as long as she could. Then she exploded.

'What's the matter with all of you?' she demanded suddenly. 'I'm not going to bite any of you. Why don't you talk and act like humans? Are you always like this when there's a woman around? No wonder you're all single! And don't think I'm going to be shocked at something you may say. Dad could out-cuss a mule skinner when something didn't go to suit him. I recall the time when an old brindle boar we had ran between his legs and upset him into a pile of manure. The things he said! It was like listening to poetry.'

The hands stared at her, open-mouthed. Then somebody chuckled. Low-voiced conversations began. Soon the voices grew louder. Another two minutes and the room was in its customary meal-time state of pandemonium.

After eating, the cowboys ducked their heads to her, grinned and trooped out. Old Dirty-Shirt chuckled long and loud.

'Looks like you've got 'em, ma'am,' he chortled, his eyes twinkling delightedly. 'Looks like they figure you belong.'

Jim Weston, who had been busy with some chore in the little room Arch Carol had used for an office, came in for a belated meal. Leah sat with him while he ate in silence. He pushed back his chair and rolled a cigarette with the slim fingers of his left hand.

'Mind if I smoke, ma'am?' he asked belatedly.

'Do you think you could spare one?' Leah asked. 'I don't smoke often, but I do like a cigarette now and then.'

Weston blinked and proceeded to manufacture a second brain tablet. Leah regarded him through the blue haze of the smoke.

'Mr. Weston,' she said, 'I imagine you were

41

thoroughly conversant with my brother's affairs. Mr. Jarrett mentioned in his letter that there was some money in the bank to the credit of the Lucky Seven.'

'There is, some,' Weston replied. 'Hardly enough, though, to see the outfit through the winter properly. We had planned to get a shipping herd together, but your brother meeting with his — accident sort of bogged things down. If we can comb out a herd in a hurry, now while the market is at a high level, we can get through the winter nicely, with money left over, but we'll have to work fast.'

'All right, work fast,' Leah said. 'And you can tell the men that if that herd is gotten together in time, there will be a bonus of a month's wages for every man.'

As had become a habit with him of late, Jim Weston looked a trifle dazed. 'Why, that's mighty fine of you, ma'am. The boys will appreciate it, and they'll have that herd ready to roll in time,' he replied.

Leah nodded. 'And now,' she said, 'I'd like to ride around a bit and look over my property, with you as a guide. I suppose you can procure me a horse?'

'Yes, I'll get one,' he replied, rising to his feet.

'And can you rake up something for me

to ride in?' Leah asked. 'I'm afraid I'd attract a good deal of attention in this dress. The skirt is tight and a trifle short.'

Weston blinked again. He ran his fingers through his black hair perplexedly. It was old Dirty-Shirt who solved the problem.

'Ma'am,' he said, 'if you don't mind, you can wear one of my shirts and a pair of coveralls. Reckon they'll fit pretty well; we're about the same size. And I got a pair of boots that'll be a mite too big, but I'll stuff paper in the toes and I reckon they'll stay on.'

'That will be wonderful, and thank you,' Leah accepted. 'I'll change while you're getting the horses, Mr. Weston.'

On his way to the horse corral, Weston paused at the bunk-house and told the hands what Leah had said about the herd and the bonus. The news was received with enthusiasm.

'By gosh, it looks like things ain't going to be so bad after all,' declared old Sam Hardy. 'Reckon we'd better start on the south pastures, eh, Jim?'

'Reckon you'd better,' Weston agreed. 'Comb out good stuff and make the holding spot about half-way between the house and the south line. And those cows will be guarded day and night.'

There was grudging admiration in Weston's eyes when Leah walked down the steps. Shirt and overalls were a good fit. Weston had to admit that what was inside the overalls made a decided difference. When Dirty-Shirt wore them, they were just overalls. But now —

Standing in the yard, saddled and bridled, were two horses. One was a rather small but strongly built bay with lines that promised speed and endurance. The other was a tall blue moros the colour of pale smoke drifting through green leaves. He was the finest-looking horse Leah had ever laid eyes on.

'Oh, what a beauty!' she exclaimed.

Jim Weston smiled at this whole-hearted appreciation of his pet saddle-horse.

'Old Ashes will do,' he said.

'The name fits him,' Leah replied. 'He does look like the ashes of a wood fire with the sunlight glinting on them.'

Weston's eyes widened a trifle at the aptness of the simile. He glanced at her in a rather puzzled way, as if seeing something he had previously missed.

'The other cayuse was your brother's favourite,' he said. 'I've a notion you'll like him; he's sort of skittish at times, but he's dependable. Your brother named him Rambler, because he was always nosing around in thickets and sliding up canyons. Want me to help you to mount?'

Leah smiled slightly. The next instant she was in the saddle, firmly seated, and gathering up the reins. Weston stared at her in grudging admiration.

'Looks like you can ride, anyhow,' he said.

'I could ride before I could walk,' Leah replied. 'Which way do we go, Mr. Weston?'

For many hours they rode across the rolling rangeland, in the shadow of tall hills, beside little streams. Weston pointed out things, explaining the habits of cattle, the importance of water in this dry land, of shade, shelter from storms and the thousand and one other things pertaining to the efficient and remunerative handling of a big ranch. Leah listened with absorbed interest, mostly in silence, and when she did ask questions, Weston was surprised at their pertinency. He wondered vaguely how this 'city' girl knew so many salient facts regarding land, its proper maintenance and the possibilities of getting the most from it.

They came to a wide stretch of fine pasture. It stretched for miles, but not a single cow grazed on the lush grass. Leah's eyes roved over the lonely expanse, a pucker between her dark brows.

'Why are there no cattle here?' she asked.

Weston shrugged. 'Looks like you should be able to tell,' he remarked condescendingly. 'It's fairly obvious. There is not water here.'

Gazing across the rangeland, he did not note the dangerous light in the big blue eyes, a light that he had noticed in the eyes of old Arch Carol when trouble was in the making for somebody.

'But the grass is very luxuriant,' Leah observed casually.

'It is,' Weston admitted.

'And the hills to the east are not far off, and their slopes are cut by wide and fairly deep hollows.'

'That's so,' he was also forced to admit. He slanted her a sideways glance, wondering what the devil she was getting at.

'So,' she concluded, 'I see no reason this land should not be made productive instead of lying useless as it is.'

'You don't!' Weston snorted. This time he was looking at her and did note the light in her eyes, and experienced a sudden uneasiness.

'No, I don't,' she repeated. 'Mr. Weston, I do not doubt but that you are a capable cattleman, but you lack imagination and vision. Did you ever in your vast experience hear of something called an artesian well?'

Weston gulped. He knew very well what was coming and realised belatedly that he had blundered into a trap. Too late now to mention that he had broached this very subject to Arch Carol more than once. Carol, competent but somewhat old-fashioned, with scant patience for new-fangled notions, had brushed Weston's suggestions aside.

'We had them on the farms in Illinois,' Leah continued. 'The condition of the grass is evidence of an underground water system here, and the contours of the hills suggest that the water reservoir is under considerable pressure. Artesian wells — two or three should be sufficient — would guarantee an adequate flow to establish streams across this land and provide cattle which would graze here with water for their needs.'

Weston said nothing, for the very simple fact that he had nothing to say. She was right on all counts. He was furious with himself, and his resentment spilled over on her. It seemed she was always one jump ahead of him.

'I suppose drilling rigs can be hired in this part of the country?' Leah suggested rather than asked.

'They can,' he admitted.

'Very well, then,' she said. 'As soon as the

work of collecting a shipping herd is finished, arrange to hire a rig and drill here.'

'All right,' Weston replied.

'And if I happen to be wrong about the subterranean pressure, although I don't think I am, we can install a few windmills and still get plenty of water,' Leah added.

Weston nodded agreement, and the subject was dropped.

CHAPTER IV

Leah was beginning to feel the effects of long hours in the saddle, after having been away from one for more than a year, but she made no complaint. However, it was a relief when Weston suggested they stop at a spring and make some coffee.

'I always pack some in my saddle-pouch, and a little flat bucket,' he explained. 'Find a steaming cup sort of sets you up after a long ride.'

'It'll be wonderful,' Leah agreed whole-heartedly.

While Weston kindled a fire, the girl wandered about, finding many novel things to interest her. She was some distance off when from a thicket ambled a big-eyed creature with wobbly legs.

'Oh, what a darling calf!' she exclaimed. She stepped forward eagerly, hand out-stretched to the little animal. Her ears were shattered by Weston's stentorian roar.

'Look out! you little fool!' he bellowed. 'Run! Run!' He was racing toward her as he spoke.

Leah heard a raucous bawl. From the thicket crashed a bony old cow, eyes glaring, needle-pointed horns lowered. Realising her danger, Leah fled for her life. Before she had taken three steps her foot plunged into a grass-grown badger hole and she fell headlong. Prone on the ground, struggling to rise but half-stunned by the fall, she saw Weston flash past her, saw him swerve, dodge the slashing points and grip the charging cow by the horns. A wrenching twist, his long body flew through the air, and the cow hit the ground with a bone-cracking thud, Weston still gripping the horns.

'Fork your horse!' he panted. 'I can't hold this infernal critter for ever.'

Leah scrambled to her feet, stumbled to where Rambler stood waiting and managed to mount him. Weston, watching from the corner of his eye, let go of the bawling struggling cow and raced for his own horse. The cow charged after him, horns lowered.

But Ashes knew exactly what to do. He danced back nimbly, weaving and ducking. Leah saw a tight loop snake out and settle over the widespread horns, just grazing the points. Ashes whirled and raced parallel to the cow, but in the opposite direction. The rope tightened with a hum like a giant harp-string. The cow turned a complete flip-flop and hit the ground again, this time with a force that knocked all the fight out of her. Weston dropped from the bull and slipped loose his twine. Without a glance at the thoroughly subdued cow that got shakily to its feet and lurched back into the thicket, he coiled the rope and hung it back on his saddle.

'Wonder if that darned fire's gone out?' he observed in conversational tones.

Leah stared at him. 'You saved my life, and risked your own to do it,' she faltered.

Weston shrugged his broad shoulders. 'All in the day's work,' he replied. 'I'd have done it for Dirty-Shirt Jones or anybody else. But don't go patting stray calfs on the rangeland; it isn't healthy here. You're not on an Illinois farm.' He squatted on his heels and began blowing up the fire.

Leah's lips tightened. She told herself that she did not like Mr. Jim Weston.

They drank the coffee in silence. Weston rolled a couple of cigarettes and handed one to Leah without comment. She accepted it with a nod. Abruptly Leah broke the silence, asking a question she had wished to ask ever since arriving in Texas.

'Mr. Weston,' she said, 'all I've been told concerning my brother's death is that he met with an accident. Can you tell me just what was the nature of that accident?'

Weston hesitated, then told her, withholding nothing. She listened in silence until he had finished.

'And the murderers were not recognised?' she asked. Weston shrugged.

'Neither the boys nor myself had ever seen any of those who were killed before,' he replied. 'We packed the bodies to town, but nobody there recognised them, or if they did, they didn't admit it.'

'Just what do you mean by that last?' Leah asked. Weston shrugged again.

'We've been plagued by outlaw depredations in this section for the past year,' he prefaced his reply. 'Cattle have been stolen, and there have been several robberies and killings. Perhaps I shouldn't say what I'm going to say, but in my opinion the outlaws are in touch with somebody who knows what goes on in the section and passes the word along to them. We've always had trouble with wide-loopers. This section is close to the outlaw country of the Big Bend and Mexico, but what's happened in the past year seems to indicate a well-organised band with somebody at the head who is shrewd and resourceful. I could be wrong in my surmise, but I don't think I am. So I figure it's just possible that somebody did recognise those hellions and kept it to himself.'

'And those who got away, of course you didn't recognise them?'

'Never got close enough to them to get a good look,' Weston replied. 'They hightailed, and our broncs were in no shape to run them down.'

'And so my brother was murdered.'

'Guess that's about the size of it,' Weston conceded. Leah was silent for a long moment; then:

'Mr. Weston,' she said, 'you would be doing me a very great favour if you could possibly learn the identity of those killers?'

'And if I do?'

'Then I think you will know just what steps to take,' Leah replied deliberately.

'Yes.'

His voice was quiet when he spoke the monosyllable, but there was a look in his pale eyes that gave the girl a sudden cold feeling around her heart. And she instinctively regretted her impulsive request, which under the circumstances amounted to an order.

Weston carefully extinguished the fire and stood up. 'Time to be heading for home,' he said. 'I imagine you've had enough for one day.'

'But I enjoyed every minute of it,' she replied.

'Even the ruckus with the cow?'

'Even that. It was the most thrilling experience of my life, and next time I'll know better.'

'Live and learn,' he said as he swung into the saddle. 'That is, if you manage to stay alive long enough.'

Leah thought that over and decided it did not require an answer.

As they neared the ranch-house in the blue and gold of the evening, she suddenly twisted in her saddle to face him.

'Mr. Weston,' she said, 'I recall Mr. Jarrett, the lawyer, saying that from now on I was to "hand out the powders." I gather it meant I was to give the orders, is that right?'

'That's right,' Weston replied uneasily.

'Well,' said Leah, 'I'm handing you one right now.'

'What?' he asked.

'Shave!' Leah snapped. Weston drew a deep breath.

'I will,' he promised.

CHAPTER V

Leah Carol meant exactly what she had said when she had told Jim Weston that she intended to learn the cattle business. She proceeded to do so, at the expense of blistered hands, sunburn, sore bones and aching muscles. From daylight till dusk she rode the range with the hands. At night she was so tired she fell asleep almost before her head touched the pillow. Grumpy old Sam Hardy had taken her under his wing and was teaching her the rudiments of roping and branding and many other things essential to the running of a cow factory. Hardy, a cowhand for more than forty years, knew just about all there was to know about the business, and he was a good teacher, with a newly developed patience that astounded the Lucky Seven cowboys, accustomed as they were to old Sam's irascible disposition and intolerance of incompetence in any form. Before three days had passed the Lucky Seven bunch definitely decided that she 'belonged'. Relations were mutually friendly. To them she was Miss Leah. To her they were Sam, Tom, Bob, Jeth, Clay.

But between her and the range boss it was 'Ma'am' and 'Mr. Weston'.

'They just don't seem to get along at all,' complained Tom Peters. 'They're all the time snappin' at each other.' The other hands nodded solemn agreement. Only old Dirty-Shirt Jones, wise in the ways of men and women, chuckled and appeared amused rather than concerned.

The second day after her arrival at the ranch Leah had sent Dirty-Shirt to town for shirts and overalls exactly the same as he wore, and for a pair of riding-boots, size three and a half.

'You were lucky, ma'am,' Dirty said when he returned with the required articles. 'Gus Rittenhouse had a pair of boots exactly the size you wanted. He ordered 'em for a gal who was visiting the Calloways and she never came for 'em. Gus says he don't regularly carry a size that small.'

'The next time you see him, tell him to order some,' Leah replied. 'I'll be wanting them.'

Dirty-Shirt had also purchased a pair of woolly chaps for brush riding.

Leah never wore anything but denims to ride in, which won the whole-hearted approval of the hands.

'She's got sense,' was the consensus of opinion. 'No fancy ridin'-pants and silk shirts for her. Just plain Levi's and cottons. Beginning to look like having a lady boss ain't so bad, after all.'

Of course the word got around. Floyd Jarrett rode to the Lucky Seven ranch-house to disprove what he thought to be but a rumour. Instead, he had it confirmed, which did not displease him.

'In my opinion you have made a wise decision, my dear,' he told Leah. 'Don't you think so, Jim?'

'Guess she's old enough to know her own mind,' Weston answered.

'And fortunate in having one of her own,' said Jarrett.

Nelson Haynes was not pleased when Jarrett acquainted him with Leah's decision. However, he was not greatly discouraged.

'She'll get tired of it when the novelty wears off,' he predicted.

'Possibly,' replied the lawyer, who believed otherwise.

Jim Weston received some disquieting news from old Sam Hardy, who had been handed the chore of tallying the cattle on the north and east pastures.

'We're losing cows,' said Hardy.

'What makes you think so?' asked Weston.

'I don't think so; I know,' replied Hardy.

'You sure?' Weston persisted.

'Listen, you ganglin' range tramp, I was punchin' cows before you were born!' exploded the irascible Hardy. 'After I've rode over a pasture I can tell you within half a dozen head how many critters are usin' it. I can darn near tell you what colour they are. And when cows I've spotted ain't there, I'll know it. We've lost better'n a hundred head in the last two or three nights.'

Weston looked sober; it was no laughing matter. Such a steady drain on an owner's resources could be serious, even more so than the occasional spectacular running off of a herd.

'Where do they go?' he asked Hardy. 'They could hardly be run clear across our range to the south, and they'd have to come south to reach the Pass.'

'They could run 'em north across Nelson Haynes' south pastures, make it through the hills by way of Clear Water Canyon, turn south and reach the Pass before daylight.'

'Yes, they could do that,' Weston conceded. 'Not likely anybody from Haynes' outfit would be down on their south pasture after dark, so they'd have little fear of being spotted.'

'Well, what we going to do about it?' demanded Hardy.

Weston rolled a cigarette and smoked thoughtfully for several minutes before replying.

'We've pretty near got the shipping herd chore licked, and a good tally of everything south of the ranch-house,' he finally said. 'A few more days will see the herd ready to roll. So I figure I can pull you and Tom Peters off for the rest of the chore. Suppose you stake out in Clear Water Canyon for a couple of nights and keep a watch on anything that happens to pass through. That way you'll get a check on how the hellions operate and we'll be all set to land on them like forty hen-hawks on a settin' quail. But if you do spot somebody, don't start a row. You'll just succeed in getting blown from under your hats and accomplish nothing worth while. I'll warn Peters. Your chore will be to get a line on what's going on, and that's all.'

'Okay,' grunted Hardy. 'You'll see Tom?'

'Yes, I'll see him,' promised Weston. 'And I'll expect you to keep him from doing anything foolish. Tom's hot-headed and might want to charge a whole outfit.'

'I'll hold the young hellion if I have to bend a gun-barrel over his thick head to do it,' Hardy declared. 'Okay, we'll set out right after dark and hole up in the canyon.'

Until he had something more definite to go on, Weston did not consider it necessary to relay to Leah what Hardy had told him. When she announced her intention of riding with the shipping herd, he offered no objections. It would be just that much more valuable experience for her.

The day before the herd was due to roll, old Sam Hardy appeared in a black rage.

'Three nights we spent in that hole freezing to death and not a single blasted cow went through!' he howled. 'And in the past two nights we lost another hundred head and more.'

'If they didn't go through Clear Water, where the devil did they go?' Weston asked.

'Where did they go!' bellowed Hardy. 'They went south, of course. You work-dodgers down here would sleep through the Crack of Doom! You let a herd pound right past you and don't hear a thing! Where did they go!'

'Hold it,' Weston told him. 'You know the shipping herd is guarded all the time. I spent the dark hours of the past three nights on a hilltop down there, from where I could see across the range for miles in every direction. Nothing passed going south, I can swear to that.'

'Then where *did* they go?' Hardy repeated Weston's question.

'I don't know,' Weston admitted. 'You sure you and Tom didn't do a little snoozing up there?'

Old Sam fairly danced with fury. 'Dadgum you, if I was forty years younger I'd larrup you within an inch of your life!' he roared.

'Take it easy.' Weston grinned. 'You know I was only joking. But just the same this business isn't a joke. At this rate we'll be bled white before the winter's over. We've got to find out how those cows got out of the valley and see to it that no more get out. I'll take seven of the boys with me on the drive. You and the others will stay here and keep a watch on things. Patrol the north pastures especially. Perhaps you can learn something, but as I said before, don't get into a row if you're badly outnumbered. Just try and learn how they get the cows out. Of course if you get a chance to crack down on somebody with the odds even, go to it.'

'That's all I ask, just a crack at the blasted thieves,' growled Hardy. 'And I'll bet that whoever it is, it's the same bunch that did for poor old Arch. Just let me get a crack at them!'

The herd was ready to roll. Almost at the last minute Jim Weston changed his plans. He had intended to ship east by railroad from Marta, but an Indian reservation agent in New Mexico, with whom Arch Carol had had dealings, telegraphed a request for good beef in a hurry, offering somewhat better than the current market price. Weston at once consulted Leah.

'It'll mean a drive of a hundred miles and more, but it'll pay off,' he told her.

'I rely on your judgment in such matters, Mr. Weston,' she replied. 'Do whatever you think best.'

'All right, New Mexico it is,' said Weston.

When Leah told him that she intended to ride with the drive, old Dirty-Shirt Jones chuckled.

'But you'll have to do whatever Jim tells you to do,' he warned. 'On a drive the trail boss is *boss*. Not even an owner can countermand his orders. That's cow country law.'

'I imagine when he gives an order it will be for the best interest of all concerned,' Leah replied.

The shipping herd rolled at daybreak, point men riding on either side of the marching column, not in front but not too far back from the head of the column, ready to swerve the leaders whenever the course was altered. Swing riders placed their horses where the herd would begin to bend in case of a change of direction, about a third of the way back from the point men. Their duties, and those of the flank riders, another third of the way back, included discouraging sideways straying and driving off any foreign cattle that might seek to join the herd. Drag riders brought up the rear, hustling along the obstinate or lazy critters that tended to fall back. Following the drag was the remuda of spare mounts. Last of all came the chuck wagon, with old Dirty-Shirt bouncing about on the high seat and spewing jovial profanity at his four horses.

The herd was a straight steer herd and less troublesome to drive than a 'mixed herd' including both cows and steers.

The route, north by slightly west, roughly followed the Paisano Trail.

Weston had mapped the route carefully, choosing the best going rather than the shortest distance to his rendezvous with the Indian agent waiting to receive the herd.

'We don't want to work the meat off them,' he explained to Leah. 'Lost weight means lost money. Better to take a little more time getting there than to hustle them along over rough country and end up with bags of bones.'

'Like me,' she smilingly replied.

Weston's face was abruptly the colour of a Texas sunset.

'Looked in the mirror lately?' he asked.

'What a question to put to a wowan!' she replied.

'Well, if you look close you'll already see a change in yourself,' he said. 'I think the Texas air agrees with you. Just a couple of weeks have already done considerable. Dirty's overalls wouldn't fit overly loose any more.'

'I hope it is an improvement,' she murmured demurely.

'It is!' Weston surprised himself with the emphasis of his reply.

It was Leah's turn to have more colour in her cheeks than was whipped there by the wind.

CHAPTER VI

The first day, Weston pushed the cattle hard, for he wanted them thoroughly tired out by nightfall, so they would be less liable to stampede or try to wander back to their accustomed feeding grounds. That night the bedding-down spot was chosen some distance west of Marta, a good twenty-five miles having been covered. From there on, ten miles a day would be the average. The long, snaky train would be abandoned and the cows would graze forward in a great arrowhead formation, the point being to the front.

Being familiar with the section, Weston did not need to scout ahead of the herd and pick out a suitable bedding spot, as it would be necessary for him to do later on. The chuck wagon did roll ahead of the herd in the late afternoon, and Dirty-Shirt had supper ready by the time the cows were bedded down for the night.

Weston advised Leah to sleep in the chuck wagon, but she vetoed the suggestion.

'Unless you order me not to, as trail boss, I'm going to sleep in a blanket on the ground like the rest of you,' she said.

'Okay with me,' Weston relented. 'It'll be your bones that'll do the aching.'

'You said yourself that they're better upholstered than they used to be,' she retorted. 'I'll take a chance on them.'

Weston grinned and said nothing more.

'At this rate, before the drive is over they may be acting like human beings towards each other, instead of a couple of Gila monsters on the prod,' old Dirty-Shirt, who had overheard the conversation, confided to Peters.

As they started out at dawn the following morning, after breakfast by lantern light, Weston cast an amused glance at the rifle butt protruding from the saddle-boot Leah had attached to her rig. She intercepted the glance.

'It isn't for show,' she said. 'I can shoot. I don't know anything about revolvers, but with a rifle I'm not at all bad. I used one on the farm as soon as I was big enough to raise it to my shoulder, and I've got good eyesight.'

'Think you're going to need it?' he asked.

'I don't know,' she replied. 'The chances are I won't, but after you telling me about what happened to Arch, I can't help but wonder if something similar might happen again somewhere. As you say, this is a valuable herd and worth a lot of money.'

'That's right,' Weston agreed soberly. 'Worth enough to cause gents with share-the-wealth notions to look it over. However, the terrain over which we'll be passing is pretty well travelled, especially till we cross into New Mexico. Also it's mostly fairly open ground and we can usually see quite a ways on all sides. That isn't favourable to wide-loopers. What you have to fear on a drive like this is a sudden swoop from under cover that catches the riders off guard; that or a provoked stampede which scatters the herd. Then it's comparatively easy for the hellions to cut out or round up a bunch and away with them. They operate where they are familiar with the ground and able to elude pursuit. But neither method works well in open country and is seldom tried where the terrain isn't favourable.'

'And we pass over no such terrain?' Leah asked.

'Not until we cross the New Mexico line,' Weston replied. 'After that, yes. But I anticipated just such a possibility and have arranged with the agent to meet us just north of the line with a bunch of his riders, as he used to do when your brother shipped to him. I notified him when to expect us. It isn't hard to estimate within a day or two, and he'll be ready.'

The fifth day out, the trail swerved sharply to round the north-east shoulder of the Baylor Range and headed north up the broad arid valley lying between the frowning rampart of the Sierra Diablo on the west and the Delaware Mountains on the east, traversing one of the most desolate yet weirdly beautiful stretches of country to be found in Texas. The view swept almost level reaches, grey-green with sage and greasewood, with here and there clumps of prickly pear, yucca and ocotillo. The blazing white streaks that were the crystal-encrusted shorelines of salt lakes gleamed like hazy silver ribbons. There were tangles of ridges and canyons where the ragged crest of the Delawares and the sheer wall of Sierra Diablo loomed stark against the sky.

'Mines in those holes, some of them working, some lost and hunted for by prospectors and desert rats,' Weston observed.

'I never dreamed anything could be so utterly wild and lovely,' Leah said. 'Beautiful as a Nightingale of Paradise singing on the

Tree of Eternity.'

'When she said that, I'll be darned if Jim didn't actually smile.' Old Dirty-Shirt chuckled. 'Maybe he's getting over his peeve. Of course he wanted the Lucky Seven bad, was mighty disappointed when he couldn't tie on to it and sort of took his spite out on her, I reckon.'

'Well, the way things are going, I've a notion that, although he doesn't know it yet, he stands a good chance of getting it,' Tom Peters replied.

Old Dirty, understanding perfectly what Peters meant, chortled with delight.

'That would be fine,' he said. 'Yes, sir, just fine!'

On the morning of the eighth day, gazing eastward, they saw the grim outline of what looked like a huge fortress which Weston knew to be the towering block of Guadalupe Peak, dominated by the sheer cliff, more than eight thousand feet in height, El Capitan.

'And right ahead,' said Weston, 'is New Mexico and some mighty bad going. I'll be glad when we meet the agent and his men. Wild country from here on and little travelled.'

'You think we might meet with trouble of some kind?' Leah asked.

Weston shrugged his broad shoulders. 'Liable to meet with anything in this section,' he replied. 'I don't really anticipate trouble, but just the same we'll be on the lookout for it. However, with the agent's riders added to our eight — nine including Dirty-Shirt — we won't have anything to worry about.'

Across the New Mexico state line rolled the herd, into a grim and desolate region of black rock and white water, hills gashed by gorges and canyons. But the going was not bad, and the trail and its approaches were always fairly wide.

However, before nightfall Weston had something to worry about. Although they were well away from Texas now, the agent and his men had not yet put in an appearance, while Weston had expected to meet them hours earlier.

'Oh, well, they must have gotten held up by something,' he told Leah. 'We'll barge into them in the morning. Nice spot for bedding-down here. Good grass and water, and the hillslopes quite a ways off.'

But the following morning was a repetition of the day before. The herd marched on between long, brush-grown ridges, past dark canyon mouths, over wider stretches of grassland, and it marched alone. No horse and rider loomed in the distance. The silence was unbroken save for the moan and thunder of swift water, the calls of birds and the passing of the herd. Weston was getting decidedly puzzled over the non-appearance of the agent and his men.

In the early afternoon he had something else disquieting to think about. His eyes were roaming the terrain ahead, marking every movement of birds on the wing, the action of little animals in the brush, the play of light and shadows on the wooded slopes. After a bit, he ambled forward to pull alongside Tom Peters, who was riding flank. Peters glanced at his face and instantly asked a question:

'Something wrong Jim?'

'I don't know, Tom, but there could be,' Weston replied. 'All afternoon there's been a jigger riding the ridge crest to the right. He's been trying to keep out of sight, but I spotted him a couple of times. Thought at first it was just a shadow, but it didn't take me long to decide otherwise.'

'Riding the ridge crest? What the devil!'

'My guess is that he's keeping tabs on us,' Weston answered. 'Don't see any other reason for him to be up there tailing us like he is.'

'Figure there's a bunch maybe down on

the opposite sag keeping pace with him?'

'Could be,' Weston conceded.

'And do you think they may swoop down on us?' Peters asked, frowning blackly.

'Hardly likely, unless they get some kind of a break,' Weston answered. 'Nine of us, not including the girl, and at that distance they wouldn't know she's a girl. No cow-lifting bunch is apt to try conclusions with nearly a dozen riders who they know will be on the lookout. What we've got to watch, if there's really anything to watch, is something unexpected, something we didn't figure on at all. We'll be careful about bedding down tonight and take precautions, although I don't think there's much danger of a night attack in such a section as this. Too hard to run cows off over such a terrain. What I'd like to know is where in tarnation is Cromwell and his riders. We sure should have met him before now. Something darned funny about this, and I can't for the life of me figure what it could be. Of course he might have been delayed, but a delay of two days and better is a bit out of ordinary. Oh, well, we'll have to make the best of it. Pass the word along to the boys, quietly, and tell them to keep their mouths shut. No sense in scaring the girl.'

'Somehow I got a notion she ain't the

scaring sort,' Peters remarked.

'Maybe not,' Weston admitted, 'but being scared or not being scared doesn't make any difference to flying lead. Darn it! I wished she'd stayed at home.'

Peters glanced at his worried countenance and stifled a grin.

Weston chose the bedding-down spot with even greater care than the evening before. He doused the fire before dark, doubled the night guard and ordered the other hands to sleep far apart in the shadow of bush or rock.

'Nothing in particular. Just not taking chances; rough country hereabouts,' he replied when Leah asked for an explanation. She nodded without comment. He had an uneasy feeling that she didn't believe him.

And then the weather gods, always a malicious and unpredictable bunch, decided to take a hand.

During the night a great purple cloudbank rolled slowly up from the south-west, veiling the stars. When morning broke, a dank wind was blowing. Not very hard, but steady, and the sky was a flattened leaden arch. The cowboys shivered as they gathered around the fire and drank scalding-hot coffee.

'Must have gotten twenty degrees colder since last evening,' Leah observed to Weston.

'Yes, it has,' he replied, 'and I sure don't like the looks of those clouds. I'm afraid we're in for a wetting. Better put your slicker on. Well, tomorrow night we should be safe in Orville, where I suppose Bill Cromwell, the agent, is holed up comfortable and has forgotten all about us, blast him!'

The herd got under way, the cattle bleating querulously, seeming to sense something they didn't like. And overhead the ominous cloud flowed steadily from the south-west, and the wind was strengthening.

With the speed and unexpectedness of a woman changing her mind, and with similar catastrophic results, it happened. A jagged flash of lightning split the sky from zenith to horizon and seemed to fall to earth in a torrent of flame. As if scorched to frantic life by those fiery fingers, the wind rose with a bellowing roar that dwarfed the boom of the thunder. And the rain fell.

'Come on,' Weston shouted to Peters. 'I want to see how things are going up front. Come on!'

They slogged their horses forward, and Leah Carol rode beside Weston.

'Get back behind the drag, in the wagon, out of this!' he cried. 'This is no place for a woman!'

Leah did not answer. Neither did she turn back. Weston swore, but the wind whipped the curses from his lips and flung them to drown in the universal tumult. He set his teeth and urged his labouring mount to greater speed.

They swept past the cursing flank riders, misty blurs in the deluge, and surged ahead.

'What was that?' Peters suddenly yelled. 'That wasn't thunder! There's another one!'

'Rifle fire!' Weston shouted back. 'Come on! Something wrong up in front. Where are the swing riders? I don't see them.'

'How can you see anything in this wet devil-smoke!' bawled Peters. 'They — look out!'

From the weaving curtain of the rain burst a terrified horse, eyes rolling, nostrils flaring, empty saddle jolting and popping.

'That's Bob Rader's horse!' howled Peters. 'What's going on ahead there? Look out!'

Five horsemen had bulged into view as the wind hurled the sheets of rain high. There was a spurt of orange flame, the whistle of a passing slug. The riders slithered to a halt.

Weston jerked his Winchester from the

saddle-boot, clamped it to his shoulder and pulled trigger as fast as his fingers could work the ejection lever. He saw a man lurch sideways and fall. Another jostled his hat on his head. All of a sudden he realised that a third rifle was booming beside him.

'You little fool!' he roared. 'Get back out of this!'

'I told you I could shoot!' Leah screamed in reply. She fired as she spoke, and a third man pitched from the saddle. The two remaining whirled their horses and went streaking back through the rain. Weston thundered after them. He saw the riders jerk to a halt, whirl again. Three more horsemen flashed into view.

The battle started all over. The combatants were misty blurs, weaving, shifting, blasting death at each other through the murk. Weston heard Peters curse viciously and knew he was hit. But his rifle continued to speak. So did the third rifle. Weston felt as if his heart were gripped by an icy hand. He tried to get in front of the girl, but she swerved her horse to one side and continued to shoot. Weston jammed cartridges into the empty magazine, flung the Winchester up again.

Abruptly he realised there was nothing to shoot at. Dimly he saw three riderless horses vanish in the wall of water. The lightning flashed. The thunder rolled. The awful voice of the wind grew louder.

'That did it!' he whooped to his companions, his voice sounding like a reedy whisper. 'They got a bellyful. Come on!'

'They raced along the bleating herd, eyes straining to pick out the point riders.

'The cows are veering to the left!' shrieked Peters. 'The sons turned them.'

'But their riders aren't following through!' Weston answered. 'Quick! Get around the leaders and start them to milling. We'll hold them here until this infernal downpour eases up. Careful now, in case those hellions take a notion to come back.'

'They won't!' boomed Peters. 'They didn't expect us to come riding up the herd. My God! They must have gone for the point and swing men, one after another!'

Weston did not answer. With a sick feeling he knew that Peters was probably right.

They reached the head of the herd. The bewildered leaders were jostling along, ducking their heads to the blast of the wind and rain, slanting toward the far slope of the canyon valley, which was less than a mile distant. Weston and Peters began battling to turn them until them would be travelling in a circle, Leah helping as best she could.

Despite the fury of the weather, it was easier than if they had been combating a stampede.

From down the far side of the swerving herd came a halloo, faintly heard above the storm.

'That's Johnson, the off-point man!' exclaimed Peters. 'Thank heaven they didn't get him, anyhow.' His voice raised in a stentorian bellow. There was an answering shout, nearer. A few minutes later, with the leaders bending back toward the advancing column, Johnson hove into view. He was almost on top of them before they could see him. His left cheek was bleeding profusely.

'But I believe the rain is letting up a bit, and the wind's falling,' Weston said. 'Hello, Ben, what happened?'

'Darned if I know for sure,' Johnson replied as he began assisting with the cows. 'Some hellions came scooting out of the rain and began throwing lead. Knocked a chunk loose from my face and creased my horse's rump. He spun around and skedaddled fast, across the canyon. Good thing for me he did, I reckon. Then I heard shooting. I doubt if the boys on the flank did in all this hullabaloo. What happened to you? I'm out of breath, yelling above this racket.'

'Tell you later,' said Weston. 'Keep shoving the cows back; they're beginning to mill.'

They were, and the storm was abating. The rain ceased almost as abruptly as it had begun. The wind dropped to a whisper; all about were little soft sounds, as if the trees were weeping silently together. The comparative quiet seemed strange after the bedlam of a few minutes before.

Weston turned to Leah. 'Ma'am, you can shoot all right,' he said, 'and you came in mighty handy, even though you did half scare the life out of me. Why do you have to go pushing into danger that way?'

'I wasn't pushing in any more than the rest of you,' she replied.

'It's our job, what we're paid for,' Weston said. 'With a woman it's different.'

'Not when it's the woman's property that's being protected,' she answered. 'I wouldn't think much of a woman who held back at such a time.'

'Oh, what's the use!' snorted Weston. 'You talk to her, Tom.'

Peters grinned, and didn't.

A horseman came into view. It was Ralph Connolley, one of the swing riders. He was hunched forward in his saddle and didn't look so good.

'Got one through the arm,' he said. 'Four hellions swooped out of the rain and commenced throwing lead at me. I was trying to fight back, but I'm scared I wouldn't have done much if all of a sudden some hombres hadn't busted loose on the other side of the herd. I never heard such shooting and yelling. Could even hear it above the thunder. The four hellions turned their cayuses and scooted out of sight the way they came. What *did* happen?'

Weston gave him the same answer he had given Johnson. 'Tell you later,' he said. 'Let's have a look at that arm. I'll help you off with your slicker. Here come the flank riders. Tom, didn't you stop one?'

'Skinned my leg is all,' said Peters. 'Nothing to bother about.'

Connolley had a hole through the fleshy part of his upper arm. It had bled considerably, but the flow was stopping. Weston bound a handkerchief around it and improvised a sling.

'That'll hold you for the time being,' he said.

Peters was talking with the flank men and the drag riders, who had put in an appearance while Weston was working on the wounded cowboy. The halted herd was spreading out to graze. The chuck wagon jolted to a stop not far off. All cast inquiring glances at Weston as he approached.

'Just what the devil was it about, Jim?' one of the drag riders asked.

'That bunch has been trailing us for days, waiting for a chance,' Weston replied. 'The storm gave them what they figured was an opportunity. They aimed to slide down each side of the herd under cover of the rain, do in the point, swing and flank riders and then be all over the drag before we caught on to what was happening. They landed on the point men, and some of them were turning the herd toward that canyon mouth over there to the left.'

'And if you hadn't decided to ride up front they very likely would have gotten away with it,' declared Peters. 'Running into us like they did threw the devils off balance, and we outshot them, with Miss Leah here doing a bang-up job of helping.'

Weston gazed across the herd.

'Come on, Tom, and a couple of you fellows,' he said. 'We might as well go back and see what happened. I'm afraid we're short a couple.'

'Guess you'd better stay here, Miss Leah,' Peters suggested.

'I'm going with you,' Leah said quietly. Peters shrugged and said no more.

Not far along the back-track they came upon three bodies sprawled grotesquely on the ground. Two saddled and bridled horses stood nearby. The third had evidently high-tailed.

Weston glanced at Leah. Her face was paper-white, but she held her head high and there was no shrinking in her eyes as she gazed at the slain outlaws.

But the blue eyes filled with tears when they found the body of Bob Rader, the murdered point rider, and a little farther on that of Gillian, the swing man.

Still farther on were the three wide-loopers who had fallen in the first fight. Their horses were grazing nearby.

Weston ordered the rigs taken off the animals, which were turned loose to graze in comfort. He knew they would be able to fend for themselves until picked up.

'Leave those dead snakes where they are,' he directed. 'We'll report what happened when we get to town. The sheriff of the county can come and look them over, if he's of a mind to.'

There were tools in the chuck wagon. Two graves were dug by the side of the trail, mounded over and wooden slab headboards set. Old Dirty-Shirt Jones, who was handy with a knife, carved the names and the dates.

CHAPTER VII

Dirty-Shirt got a fire going despite the wetness and dished out hot food and steaming coffee.

'Well, we might as well get them moving,' said Weston. 'Quite a few hours of daylight yet. And this isn't a good bedding-down spot.'

'Do you think those men will follow us and try to take revenge for those we killed?' Leah asked apprehensively.

'Nope,' Weston replied. 'That sort don't go out of their way to take revenge for anybody. All they think about is their own hides, and they don't risk them when there's nothing to gain. Well, let's get going. I'd hoped we'd make Orville early tomorrow, but after this delay we'll be lucky to get there by dark.'

It was nearly dark when the herd rolled into Orville the following day. Weston at once repaired to the agent's office.

'What's the big notion?' demanded Cromwell, staring in astonishment at Weston. 'You wire me you can't make it here till next week; then you come through the hills by yourself and get here today!'

'I didn't send you any wire,' Weston replied.

'Well, somebody sent one,' said Cromwell. 'Here it is.'

Weston took the telegram and glanced at it. It contained exactly what Cromwell had said it did. He gazed at the agent, his black brows drawing together.

'Well, take a load off your feet and tell me what the devil it means,' said Cromwell.

Weston sat down, rolled a cigarette and gave him a terse account of what had happened on the trail to the south. Cromwell swore explosively.

'A wonder any of you got out of it alive,' he growled. 'That was a slick scheme, all right.'

'And I think,' Weston said thoughtfully, 'that it was hatched in Marta.'

'In Marta?'

'Yes. That wire was sent, of course, to keep you from convoying us through the hills. Somebody rode ahead of us to line up a bunch here in New Mexico. Or else the bunch that has been raising the devil down around Marta rode ahead to the hills and waited their chance.'

Cromwell shook his head. 'Mighty funny thing for them to do,' he commented. 'Doesn't seem likely that a wide-looping bunch would trail a herd for better'n a hundred miles on the chance of grabbing it. No percentage there.'

'Strikes me sort of that way, too,' Weston admitted. 'But the wire was sent from Marta, which undoubtedly means the whole thing was figured out there. Wide-loopers don't commonly send messengers a hundred miles to inform other owlhoots that a herd is coming they might tie on to. Looks like somebody was mighty anxious to have this particular herd grabbed.'

'Those cows mean quite a bit of money,' Cromwell observed.

'Yes, it would have been almost a crippling loss for the Lucky Seven, conditions being what they are at present,' Weston answered.

Cromwell shot him a shrewd glance. 'Know anybody who might profit from the Lucky Seven being crippled?' he asked.

Weston shook his head. 'It's beyond me,' he admitted.

'Oh, well!' grunted the agent. 'Anyhow, you got through, and that's all that matters.'

'Except that two good men were done in by the snake-blooded devils,' Weston said.

Cromwell nodded soberly. 'Well, I suppose your men are running the critters into the corral,' he remarked. 'I'll walk over there with you and take a look at them. Mighty glad to get them; takes me off a spot. Somebody blundered at headquarters, and we're mighty short of beef.'

'Okay,' agreed Weston. 'And I want you to meet the owner. She insisted on coming along.'

'She?'

'I informed you in my telegram that Arch Carol was dead and that his sister had inherited the spread,' Weston reminded him.

'Oh, of course, but I'd hardly have expected a woman her age to be riding with a herd.'

Weston smiled slightly. 'Well, she did,' he said. Having a sense of humour, he made no mention of Leah's age. He wanted to see Cromwell's reaction.

It was all he anticipated. Nor did Tom Peters' graphic account of the fight with the wide-loopers lessen the flabbergasted agent's bewilderment. Peters had the gift of gab and knew how to tell a story well.

'Ma'am,' said Cromwell, 'I've a notion you and I are going to do a lot of business in the future. Yes, there are a few nice fat contracts I figure I can throw your way. Got a place to stay tonight, no? Jim, we'll put her up at the Astor House. It isn't exactly the one in New York, but it isn't bad. The owner's a friend of mine. Ready to go, Miss Leah?'

'Yes, and I'll appreciate a real bed for a change,' the girl replied. 'Sleeping on the ground gets, well — monotonous, even though it doesn't make my bones ache,' she added with a sideways glance at Weston, who glowered.

'Come on,' said Cromwell, not noting this bit of by-play. 'Come along, Jim; you have to sleep somewhere, too. And I've a notion you had all better stick around Orville till the sheriff gets here and looks over those bodies. Chances are he'll want to talk with you. I'll wire him right away.'

At the Astor House which, while perhaps a shade less ostentatious than the famous New York hostelry of that name, appeared clean and comfortable, the white-haired old proprietor greeted them cordially.

'The very best for a friend of mine, Clate,' said Cromwell.

'Always the best for a friend of yours, Bill,' the owner said. 'Although,' and he bowed gallantly to Leah, 'such a charming lady would get the best anyhow. Where to eat? Well, the Sunset Saloon, across the way, puts out about the best chuck in town.'

'What a pretty name for a saloon,' observed Leah.

'Well,' said Clate, 'the feller it's named for ain't exactly purty, but he's a good Injun. Never-Sweat Mathers, the owner, has got red hair, so some folks called him Sunset. He figured the name would do when he opened up his snake-juice joint. So she's the Sunset. Reckon the jiggers who spend a lot of time there are more apt to see it rise than set.'

'Sounds interesting,' Leah laughed.

'Oh, it is, sometimes, but it's best not to be there when it's most interesting,' said Clate. 'Sort of unhealthy at times. Not this early in the evening, though, so I reckon you can take a chance on it, ma'am. You'll take her over, Jim?' Weston nodded.

'Give me half an hour to freshen up a bit,' Leah told him. 'I'll hurry — I'm starved.'

Old Clate led Leah upstairs to the room he had assigned her. Weston and Cromwell sat down in the little lobby and smoked.

'Didn't happen to go through those hellion's pockets down on the trail, did you?' the agent suddenly asked.

'No, why should I?' Weston asked.

'Because if your theory that they belonged to a Marta bunch is correct, you might have found something to tie them up with somebody around Marta,' the agent replied.

'I never thought of that,' Weston admitted. 'Guess I wouldn't make a very good range detective,' he added with a smile.

'Maybe the sheriff will find something, though I doubt it,' said Cromwell. 'He's a good jigger, but like most of the specimens we get in office hereabouts — quick on the draw and slow on the think tank. Well, I'm going back to the office. Tomorrow we'll run the critters across the scales and settle our business. Not too early, though. I've a notion your boys will want a little bust after all they've been through, and this is a lively pueblo. They have money? If not, I'll advance you some for them.'

'Yes, they're heeled,' Weston replied. 'The owner handed them a bonus of a month's wages each before we started the drive, for getting the herd together in time.'

'She's a real gal, all right,' chuckled Cromwell. 'A lot like old Arch, but a sight easier to look at. So long; see you tomorrow.'

Shortly after the agent took his departure, Leah came down. Weston stared at her.

'Where'd you get that dress?' he asked.

'I brought it with me, along with some

other things, in the chuck wagon, just in case I might need it,' she explained. 'Glad I did. Like it?'

'Why — it's real pretty,' Weston replied.

Perhaps Leah read the admiration in his glance, for her colour heightened and her dark lashes veiled her eyes for a moment. However, when she spoke the question she asked was prosaic enough:

'When do we eat? I told you I'm starved.'

When they entered the big saloon across the street from the hotel, Leah gazed with interest at the novel scene. When she ate with Weston in the Marta saloon only an early afternoon sprinkling of customers was being accommodated. But the Sunset was uproariously crowded. Men lined the bar from end to end, two deep. Cards slithered softly. Two roulette wheels whirred. Dice skipped across the green cloth like spotty-eyed devils. The faro bank was going strong. The orchestra was blaring, the dance-floor doing plenty of business. From the kitchen drifted rich and savoury smells.

As Leah and Weston passed through the swinging doors the uproar died to a hum. It was some moments before it resumed.

'Men are funny,' Leah remarked, after they had occupied a table and given their order to a waiter. 'The dance-floor is full of pretty girls, but let a strange, skinny wench come in and every head turns.'

Weston frowned blackly. 'Aren't you ever going to forget that?' he stormed.

'Forget what?' she asked, all innocence.

'You're not a skinny wench any more and you know it!' he said.

'Oh!' she replied. 'Nice of you to have noticed.'

His frown grew blacker. 'Sometimes,' he said darkly, 'I think you know something of such refinements of cruelty as were practised by Caligula.'

'Caligula?' she repeated. 'A Roman emperor, was he not? If you are in the mood to delve into the past, perhaps you will recall Louis the Eleventh, who had a certain churchman he didn't like put in a cage too short for him to stand erect, too narrow for him to stretch out full length. It is said he would stand for hours contemplating his victim's contortions.'

'Now what do you mean by that?' Weston demanded.

'If you will glance back over your attitude for the past month, perhaps you will find the answer, Mr. Weston,' she replied.

Weston flushed. 'I'm sorry, ma'am,' he said. 'Maybe I haven't been exactly nice. By the way, in this section of the country it's customary for an owner to call the range boss by his first name.'

'I will, if you'll stop "ma'aming" me all the time as if I were a schoolteacher,' she snapped. 'I happen to have a first name, too.'

Weston struggled with a grin, but couldn't suppress it. 'All right — Leah,' he said.

'That's better — Jim. Thank goodness here comes our dinner. I'm absolutely famished.'

Quite some time later, Weston remarked, 'Rather a rough place for you to be in.'

'I like it,' she replied. Her eyes roved over the dance-floor.

'Is it permissible for anybody to dance?' she asked.

'Of course. That's what the floor's there for.'

'Well,' she smiled, 'shall we dance?'

'Guess we could do worse.' He chuckled. 'Let's go!'

Jim Weston liked to dance, and he danced well. And in this small, flower-faced girl he found a skilful partner. Admiring glances were cast in their direction, and at the bar Big Tom Peters chuckled with delight.

'Darned if I don't believe they're getting together at last,' he observed to Dirty-Shirt.

'Was just a matter of time,' said the cook. 'Did you ever see a finer-looking couple?

Looks like the old Lucky Seven got a lucky break.'

CHAPTER VIII

Tom Peters sauntered along the bar of the Sunset to join Weston. 'Boss go to bed?' he asked.

'Yes,' Weston replied. 'She was tired.'

'And I've a notion that ruckus down on the trail is still having an effect on her,' said Peters. 'She went white when that sidewinder she plugged tumbled out of his hull. Guess it was the first time she ever shot a man.'

'Yes, I guess it was,' Weston agreed.

'Well, between you and me, if she hadn't, I've a notion one of us would have gotten it,' said Peters. 'That hellion was lining sights.'

'I believe you're right,' Weston replied soberly.

They had a couple of drinks together; then Peters wandered off to engage one of the dance-floor girls in conversation. Weston said a few words to the other hands, then retired to the end of the bar. He was so occupied with his own thoughts that he didn't hanker for company.

The Sunset was growing noisier by the minute. Weston finally tired of the incessant din. He finished his drink and sauntered out. He could always think better in the open air and figured a walk about the town might help. He strolled along the crooked main street. Absorbed in his own thoughts, he gave scant heed to what went on around him. He did not notice the three men who drifted along in his wake, slowing their gait when he slowed, quickening it when he happened to step out briskly.

One was a huge man, broad of shoulder, thick of chest and waist, a stunted Hercules run to breadth and brawn. He planted his feet solidly and swaggered as he walked. Little could be seen of his face because of the hat drawn low over his eyes and a bristle of black beard that grew almost to his cheekbones. Of the other two, one was fairly tall and well set up. He, too, was bearded but his short stubble was of a reddish hue. The third, also unshaven, boasted a scraggly growth of a couple of weeks. He was short and scrawny with quick, furtive movements. In the shadow of his hat-brim his eyes darted from side to side, rover ahead, slanted back over his shoulder. Altogether an unsavoury trio. They never let Jim Weston get out of their sight, and as he left the better section of the town and sauntered aimlessly toward the waterfront section that straggled along the north-west bank of the Sacramento river, they quickened their pace to close the distance between them and the man they followed.

Weston paused in front of a dimly lighted saloon with dirty windows. Perhaps another drink would help his thinking. He entered the saloon.

Once inside, he realised it was not exactly a prepossessing place. It was shadowy, with inadequate lighting provided by one big hanging lamp. The conversation at the bar and the gaming tables was a low hum; the girls on the dance-floor were a slatternly lot. Caution said get out; but Jim Weston wasn't in a cautious mood. He walked to the bar and ordered a drink.

The bartender, who had an observant eye, was civil enough, pouring the drink, accepting payment with a mumble of thanks and walking away.

Weston was sipping his drink when the three men who had been tailing him entered the saloon. They paused just inside the swinging doors to glance about. Then they headed purposefully toward the bar, the squat giant in front, the other two dropping back a few paces and fanning out. Weston turned at a touch on his elbow to face the big man with the thick, short beard.

'Texas?' the fellow rumbled.

'That's right,' Weston replied. Instantly he was on his guard. That question sometimes meant trouble.

'Thought so,' said the other, his hand dropping casually toward his belt. Instinctively, Weston's hand also dropped. The big man leapt back a pace with surprising agility for one of his bulk.

'No you don't!' he shouted. His right hand blurred with amazing speed toward the gun swinging at his hip. Jim Weston's right shoulder hunched a trifle.

The two reports blended almost as one, but not quite. The Texan's gun wisped smoke first by a split second.

Weston reeled sideways as a slug tore through the flesh of his upper left arm. The big man gave a queer little grunt. His gun clattered to the floor, and he lurched forward slowly, like a falling tree. Weston's bullet had caught him dead centre. With yells of fury his companions went for their guns.

Weston leaped forward, flung his bleeding left arm about the dying giant's neck and whirled him sideways to form a shield. The man's body jerked as two bullets hammered it. Weston fired over his shoulder, and the scrawny man gave a yelp of pain. Weston's gun muzzle tipped up and blasted the big hanging lamp to fragments of broken glass. Darkness swooped down like a thrown blanket.

Instantly there was utter and complete pandemonium. Yells, curses, screeches from the dance-floor girls, a smashing of furniture and a clang-jangle of falling bottles filled the air. Two guns blazed through the darkness, but Weston wasn't where he had been an instant before. He didn't make for the swinging doors as he knew the two gunmen would expect him to do. Instead, he streaked across the room in the opposite direction, his gun-barrel flailing right and left. When he entered the place he had noticed a second door in the back. He headed for that door, praying it wouldn't be locked. He fell over a smashed chair, floundered to his feet, gripping his gun tight, and immediately hit the floor again via an overturned table. He slammed into somebody, struck out hard with the gun-barrel and felt it crunch against flesh and bone. The next thing he slammed into was the back wall. He fumbled along it, searching frantically for the doorknob, found it.

The door wasn't locked. He flung it open, slipped through and slammed it shut behind him. The thud of a bullet into the boards synchronised with the muffled boom of a gun inside the saloon, which was boiling and bubbling with sound like a giant pot. Weston went up what appeared to be a dark alley at a dead run, still gripping his gun, blood pouring from his wounded arm and dripping from his fingertips. Shortly he turned a corner into a better-lighted section, got his bearings and proceeded at a fast pace. He wanted to get to his room as quickly as possible, for his wounded arm was badly in need of attention. In his saddle-pouches were rolls of bandages with which he could staunch the flow of blood, which was heavy enough to be alarming. Already he was conscious of the slight haziness that accompanies excessive loss of blood.

There were not many people on the street, and those who were there paid no attention to him. Passing through the deserted lobby of the hotel, he stumbled up the stairs. Sagging against the closed door, he strove to unlock it, fumbling awkwardly with the key. While he was making the vain attempt, the door across the hall opened a crack and

Leah peered out.

'What's the matter, Jim?' she asked. 'Oh, good heavens! Your hand is covered with blood! What happened?'

'Got one through the arm,' he mumbled. 'Can't see to open the infernal door.'

She sped across the hall, took the key from his ineffectual fingers and thrust it into the lock. Flinging open the door, she supported him into the room and to a chair.

'Bandages in saddle-pouches,' he said. 'Will you get them, please? I feel a mite tuckered.'

'You stay where you are,' she ordered. She dumped the contents of the pouch on to the bed, secured the rolls of bandage. Working with swift, sure hands, she stripped off his shirt. The wound was a ragged tear from which blood flowed profusely.

'Bone's not broken, is it?' she asked. Weston shook his head.

'A vein wound, not arterial,' she said. 'I think I can stop the flow with pads. Bad place for a tourniquet, even if I wanted to use one. Save that as a last resort. Improperly handled, it can be dangerous.'

Weston did not argue the point. He was dimly conscious of her capable hands padding and bandaging his arm, of her thumb and finger applying pressure at just the right spot.

'You seem to know a good deal about such things,' he muttered.

'When you spend all your life on a farm, you learn to take care of injuries,' she replied. 'There, I believe that's got it. The flow has slackened greatly. Yes, that will do. Would you like me to roll you a cigarette?'

'Paper and tobacco in the shirt pocket,' he mumbled. 'Can you?'

'I used to roll them for Dad,' she replied. 'There, how's that? I'm going to improvise a sling from the shirt, until I can rake up something better. I think you'd better stay in the chair, if you feel up to it, rather than lie down.'

A makeshift sling was quickly forthcoming and the arm placed in an easy position. Leah stepped back and nodded with satisfaction.

She headed for the door. Before reaching it, she paused.

'Wait,' she said. 'You need hot coffee and a lot of it, after losing all that blood. I'll slip on a dress and get some from the saloon across the way.'

'Not at this time of night, you mustn't,' he objected.

'I'll be all right,' she answered. 'The boys

are over there, aren't they?'

Weston continued to protest feebly, for talking required some effort, but she paid no heed. Glancing up and down the hall, she sped across to her room. A few moments later he heard her pattering down the steps.

There were stares aplenty when Leah entered the saloon alone, but she ignored them and hurried to where Peters and Dirty-Shirt were standing together at the bar. In a few swift words she told them what she wanted and why.

'You get it, Tom,' she concluded. 'I'm going back to Jim.'

'I'll go with you,' said Dirty-Shirt. 'Get a move on, Tom.'

Very quickly Peters came pounding up the stairs with a bucket of coffee, still bubbling, and a mug.

'Get on the outside of this, Jim,' he said, brimming the mug with the steaming liquid.

Weston accepted the coffee and sipped it thirstily.

'And now can you tell us what happened?' asked Peters.

Weston told them, tersely but in detail. Peters swore under his breath.

'A pity you didn't gut-shoot all three of 'em,' he growled. 'So they were aiming to sort of even up for what happened down on the trail.'

'Maybe,' Weston conceded dubiously. 'But it was a mighty queer deal. They knew exactly who they were looking for, and they came in to do a killing, no doubt of that. I'm of the opinion that the big jigger was a professional gun-fighter — he was mighty fast — and planned to make it look like I started the ruckus, figuring he could beat me to the pull and there would have been fifty hellions in that hole to swear I reached first. Cowhands, contrary to the popular impression, are seldom good shots or fast on the draw. Of course there are exceptions.'

'Yes,' Peters agreed dryly. 'Whoever sicked him on you didn't know you over-well. Any old-timer down around Marta could have told him he was mighty likely to bust up a dull day for the undertaker. And you think there was more to it than just a try at evening up the score?'

'I don't know, Tom,' Weston replied, 'but it was funny. Wide-loopers seldom go in for a deliberate killing unless there's something to gain, and what would they have gained by downing me?'

Peters had to echo Weston's remark, 'I don't know.'

'Jim, do you think somebody will try to

make trouble for you for killing that — what Tom just called him?' Leah asked. Peters chuckled. Weston grinned and replied:

'Highly unlikely. By the time the sheriff gets there — if he's told about it — the chances are there won't even be a body around. "Sure there was a fight in here, started by a blasted Texan, but the feller who got plugged wasn't hurt bad; he got up and walked out." That's about the answer he'll get.'

'Wouldn't be surprised if you're right,' agreed Peters.

'And now Jim had better go to bed,' Leah decided. 'If you get to feeling bad during the night, I'm right across the hall. Don't hesitate to call me. I won't go to bed until you promise.'

'I promise,' Weston replied. Leah nodded to the others and retired to her room.

'What a gal!' chuckled Tom Peters. 'Anybody says working for a lady boss ain't all right is going to get punched in the nose. You okay, Jim? Fine! See you tomorrow.'

CHAPTER IX

The following morning Weston's arm was stiff and sore and he was a trifle weak but fairly fit. Leah changed the bandage and concluded the wound was doing nicely. Weston vetoed her suggestion that a doctor be called to look at it.

'He couldn't do any more than you've done,' he declared. 'I'll be all set to start back home tomorrow.'

The sheriff, a grizzled former cowhand, showed up shortly after breakfast. He listened attentively to the account of the recent hectic happenings and nodded his approval.

'A good chore, a couple of good chores,' he said. 'Hope you come back soon, Weston, and keep up the good work. Yes, I'll ride down and look over what the coyotes and buzzards left. No sense in it, but I reckon I'm supposed to. That rumhole by the river? No use in wasting time on that. I wouldn't learn anything there. Everybody would have been home in bed when it happened. I've had experience with that sidewinders' nest before. See you this evening when I get back.'

The cattle were weighed and paid for. Cromwell, the agent, rubbed his hands complacently as he looked them over.

'A fine lot of beef,' he said. 'This eases the situation. Now my "children" will eat and not go raiding. Keep their bellies full and they're happy and peaceful. No trouble at all. I'll get in touch with you later in the year, Miss Carol, and we'll talk some more business.'

That afternoon Leah walked around the town alone. There were quite a few Mexican families, and in front of each adobe or clapboard shack was a small but well-kept garden. She paused before one where roses bloomed. A smiling Mexican woman came out of the house to greet her. Gazing at the roses, Leah asked a question, explaining why she asked it.

'*Si!*' replied the Mexican woman. 'It will be the great pleasure. No! No! you cannot pay. It will be indeed the pleasure.'

When Leah left the garden she carried a large bundle wrapped in very wet gunnysacking. She deposited the bundle in the chuck wagon.

'Keep it damp till I'm ready for it,' she told old Dirty-Shirt, who promised to do so.

It was late when the sheriff and his deputies got back from their ride down the trail.

'We took some good guns off the sidewinders, and quite a bit of money, which will go into the county treasury, I reckon, unless you fellers want to claim it as reward money,' the sheriff told Weston.

'Guess we can do without that kind of money,' Weston replied. 'Nothing else of interest?'

'Nope. That sort never carries anything of interest. We shoved 'em down a crack in the rocks and piled some brush over them. Reckon that will hold them till Judgment Day. Rounded up the horses. Good nags with Mexican skillet-of-snakes brands, which don't mean anything. I noticed the rigs were Texas rigs, but that don't mean much either in this section, where they're pretty much in use. Well, be seeing you.'

The Lucky Seven outfit set out for home early the next day. When they reached the two lonely graves beside the trail, Leah called a halt. From the chuck wagon she took the mysterious package she had stowed there the day before, dropped on her knees beside the graves and went to work. When she straightened up, wiping the caked earth from her hands, at the head of each grave was planted a small rose bush, the blooms still dewy-fresh.

Jim Weston gazed for a long moment, then turned away without a word. Big, rough Tom Peters blew his nose with great violence and mumbled something about the blasted cigarette smoke getting into his eyes.

'A gal to ride the river with!' old Dirty-Shirt Jones murmured under his breath. 'Jim Weston, if you don't grab her off, your head's full of rocks!'

The troop rode on.

The trip back to Marta and the Lucky Seven Ranch was made in good time and without incident. The cowboys were still somewhat depressed by the killing of two of their number, but swift death is too common to the rangeland to make a lasting impression. Their spirits rose as they drew near their home grounds, and they finally trooped into the bunk-house in a festive mood.

'I enjoyed it greatly, but it's good to get home,' Leah said.

'Yes,' Jim Weston agreed, 'good to get home.'

'How's your arm?' she asked.

'Just about forgot I had one.' He grinned. 'You're a swell doctor.'

Without delay, Weston had a talk with Sam Hardy.

'How'd things go?' he asked.

'Everything hunky-dory,' replied the old cowboy. 'Funny, but we didn't lose a cow while you were gone. Maybe the hellions caught on we were layin' for them and figured to pull in their horns for a while.'

'Maybe,' Weston conceded, his eyes thoughtful.

'Fact is, nobody hereabouts has lost any cows of late,' continued Hardy. 'That is, nobody but Nelson Haynes.'

'Haynes been losing cows?'

'That's right. Lost more than two hundred head, he says. He was over to the sheriff's office sounding off about it. Seemed mighty put out. I've a notion Haynes squeezes a dollar till the eagle squawks.'

'Perhaps that's how he got where he is,' suggested Weston.

'Maybe,' said Hardy with emphasis.

'Now just what do you mean by that, Sam?' Weston asked.

'Jim, I don't know,' Hardy admitted. 'Haynes has always been civil enough to me, but somehow I never could like the jigger. Can't say why, but I just don't like him.'

'Arch Carol didn't like him, either,' Weston observed.

'Arch always had plenty of savvy,' remarked Hardy. 'What do *you* think of him, Jim?'

'Why, I don't know,' Weston replied. 'Fact is, I never gave him much thought. I was sort of ruffled when I figured he was going to bid against me for the Lucky Seven and would very likely outbid me, but I really couldn't hold that against him. It was strictly a business matter. And that's all over now.'

'Maybe,' grunted Hardy. 'Nelson Haynes has always struck me as the sort of jigger who doesn't give up easy. What he wants he usually gets, one way or another.'

Tom Peters, who was present, gave a loud laugh. 'Haynes would need a couple of "ways" and about three "anothers" this time,' Peters declared. 'He's got about as much chance of getting the Lucky Seven as a terrapin has of growing feathers.'

Old Sam twinkled his shrewd old eyes at Peters.

'Tom,' he said, 'according to folks who ought to know what they're talking about, once upon a time a terrapin, or his first cousin, did grow feathers.'

'Now what the devil are you talking about,

you loco old coot?' demanded Peters.

'Just that the first bird started out as a reptile, and a terrapin is a reptile,' Hardy replied.

'Jim, do you know what he's talking about?' asked Peters.

'Well, in a way he's right,' Weston acceded. 'Evolutionists maintain, and have pretty conclusively proven, that the primal ancestor of all birds a few million years back was a reptile.'

'Set 'em up in the next alley,' grunted Peters. 'And that's just about how long it'll take Nelson Haynes to tie on to the Lucky Seven,' he added triumphantly.

The next morning Weston announced his intention of riding to town and arranging for a drilling rig.

'If we're going to sink those wells on the north pasture, we'd better get busy before the cold weather sets in,' he explained to Leah.

'You're right,' she agreed. 'Now that we've got the money to do it, there's no sense in putting it off.'

That afternoon the Lucky Seven had a visitor, an unexpected visitor. Nelson Haynes rode up to the ranch-house and introduced himself to Leah.

'Figured it was about time I paid my

respects to my new neighbour,' he said. 'Should have done it before now, but I've been mighty busy, what with the round-up coming on, trying to run down wide-loopers, and so forth.'

Leah invited him in for coffee, and they talked for more than two hours.

'Of course I was a bit disappointed at not being able to buy the Lucky Seven — it would round out my holdings nicely — but I'm rapidly becoming less disappointed,' Haynes said with his ingenuous smile.

'Why, I thought it was Mr. Weston who wanted to buy the property,' Leah replied.

'Oh, I guess he did,' Haynes said. 'But I imagine I would have been able to outbid him. Floyd Jarrett was out to get all he could for his client, yourself, for which you can't blame him. We all felt sure you'd sell and reacted accordingly. It was quite a surprise to all of us when you announced your decision to run the spread. You seem to be doing all right.'

'Mr. Weston is experienced and extremely capable,' Leah explained.

Haynes' smile tightened a trifle. 'There is no doubt as to that,' he agreed. 'Weston is very capable. I don't know him very well, but he struck me as being intelligent and efficient, decidedly so. You're fortunate in having such an employee to shoulder the responsibilities until you get the hang of things.'

Leah was not inclined to argue the point. Haynes turned the conversation into other channels.

'I'll certainly be back soon, if I may,' he said on taking his leave.

'You'll always be welcome, Mr. Haynes,' Leah replied, and meant it.

Leah informed Jim Weston of Haynes' visit when he returned from town.

'He appears to have a high opinion of your ability,' she concluded.

'Oh, Nelson is all right, I guess,' Weston replied. 'He rubs the old-timers the wrong way with his progressive notions and his impatience with their old-fashioned methods, some of which, I must concede, are a bit slipshod.'

'It's a wonder you don't rub them the wrong way, too,' Leah said. 'You could hardly be termed backward yourself.'

'Perhaps I use a different approach.' He smiled. 'It's possible to disagree with a person without making it too obvious and getting his bristles up.'

CHAPTER X

The Lucky Seven dropped back into its orderly routine. In another two weeks the fall or beef round-up would start, including all the ranches in the vicinity of Marta, and preparations were made for this all-important event. The drilling rig arrived, and Weston and the drill crew boss decided on the best places to sink the wells.

Five days after the first drill bit chugged into the soil, a well came in, sending a stream of sparkling water twenty feet into the air. Weston eyed it with satisfaction.

'Yes, two more like it will do the chore, just as we figured,' he told the driller. 'Then run some ditches and dig out holes and we'll be all set. Leah, your suggestion paid off; you're to be complimented.'

'Thank you, Jim,' she replied demurely. 'When I made it, you seemed to be quite put out.'

'Because you beat me to it and made me

look stupid,' he answered cheerfully. 'Gave me a bit of a jolt, but by now I'm so used to that happening I don't mind.'

Leaving the well and its silvery plume flashing in the sunlight, they rode south by slightly west. On the near bank of the creek they paused before sending their horses splashing through the fairly broad stream.

'How many ranches down there?' Leah asked, gesturing to the south-west.

'Five altogether,' Weston replied. 'The H F Bar, the Five Dot, the EJ, the Triangle A and the Lazy Flying E. You'll meet the owners at the round-up.'

'And what's to the south?'

'A desert. Our grassland peters out beyond our south pastures. Nothing down there for miles but sand and cactus and some greasewood and sage. Dry as the front yard of the infernal regions.'

'And suppose the creek flowed due south instead of south-west?' she asked.

'It would lose itself in the lower desert,' Weston said. 'However, its natural channel is south-west.'

'I see,' Leah said thoughtfully.

When they reached the ranch-house they found Nelson Haynes awaiting their arrival.

'Was out looking over my south pasture and thought I'd ride on down,' he said.

Leah made him welcome and invited him to stay for dinner. Haynes accepted the invitation with alacrity.

When they foregathered in the living-room later, Haynes did most of the talking, but in such a genial and entertaining manner that he did not appear to be monopolising the conversation. Jim Weston could express himself very well when he took a notion, but listening to Haynes' free and easy flow of speech, he felt constrained, almost inarticulate. Nelson Haynes was a smooth talker, and a convincing one.

Leah listened with flattering attention. After Haynes said good night and the door closed after him, she said to Weston:

'I don't think I ever met a more persuasive speaker. He reminds me of what I once read of Talleyrand, who evidently had a similar gift with which he swayed men, empires — and women.'

'And women,' Weston repeated with something of a growl in his voice. 'I recall reading that his favourite weapon was the double-cross.'

Leah laughed merrily. 'I didn't mean to compare Mr. Haynes to Talleyrand,' she protested; 'comparisons are odious. I merely commented on, and strove to illustrate, his somewhat unique ability as a conversationalist.'

Her eyes grew thoughtful. 'I wonder,' she said, 'if you also noticed that while Mr. Haynes talked a great deal, he didn't say anything.'

'Now what the devil do you mean by that?' demanded the bewildered range boss.

The blue eyes danced. 'Good night, Jim,' she said, and trotted up the stairs.

Chapter XI

It was round-up time, and Leah had elected to accompany Weston on his tour of inspection.

For half a dozen miles and more they rode at a fair pace. Weston constantly scanned the thickets, brakes and washes.

'The boys are doing a good chore of combing,' he observed at length. 'Mighty few strays. Strays mean careless combing, and I've impressed on them I don't want any of that. Yes, they're doing all right.'

'We're on Estes Shrigg's holdings now, the Lazy Flying E,' he added a little later. 'Over there to the right is our creek.'

'And the one which flows across Mr. Haynes' land?'

'You can't see it from here; it's farther to the west but pursues the same general direction.'

The sun was low in the west when they climbed a long and gentle rise to its crest.

They pulled up in the shadow of some trees to give the horses a breather. The far sag was much steeper than the one they had traversed, and brush-grown, tumbling down to a winding ribbon of trail flanked on either side by thick chaparral, its general trend almost due south, although below where they sat it flowed from the north-west.

'Where does that road go?' Leah asked.

'It's called the Terlingua Trail and runs south to the quicksilver mines,' Weston replied. 'Passes gold and silver mines, too, but quicksilver is the important output down there.'

Leah gazed south by east, following the windings of the track. 'Cattle coming this way,' she remarked. 'A good lot of them, too.'

'Some that's been combed from Shrigg's holdings, the chances are,' Weston replied. He watched the herd rolling up from the south and frowned his disapproval.

'They're pushing them too fast,' he said. 'No sense in running the fat off them that way. Guess they're in a hurry to get in for supper. I'll have a few words to say to the gents this evening.'

He eyed the dozen or so riders galloping behind the herd, his expression growing slightly puzzled.

'How the devil did so many of them get down in that section?' he demanded, thinking out loud. 'They should have been more scattered. Something else to speak to them about.'

Leah was watching the swift approach of the herd. 'Jim,' she suddenly exclaimed, 'I believe those cattle are running away.'

Weston gazed with puckered lids. 'Darned if I don't think you're right,' he agreed. 'Those terrapin-brained jugheads! Slapping their hats and slickers won't do any good — just make the cows go faster. They can't get in front of the herd to turn the leaders because of the brush on both sides of the trail, but they're acting like they were loco.'

'Here comes something else, from the other direction,' Leah said.

Weston followed the direction of her gaze and saw a huge, clumsy-looking vehicle drawn by six horses rolling down from the north-west at a fast pace.

'The Terlingua stage,' he said. 'Makes the run south every other day. Guard on the seat with the driver. Must be packing a valuable shipment of some kind. Say! There's liable to be a ruckus down there if somebody doesn't pull up.'

Directly below where they sat their horses, some four hundred yards distant, the trail curved sharply. And toward the bend of the curve raced the herd and the stage, from opposite directions.

Weston started to shout a warning, but the distance was too great. He hesitated, reached for the Winchester snugged in the saddle-boot. A slug thrown in front of the stage horses might cause the driver to pull up. Too late! The stage had flashed behind a bristle of taller brush and for the moment was hidden from view. It came in sight again, swerving around the apex of the curve. And around the bend from the opposite direction boomed the stampeding herd. Maddened cows and unprepared stage met head-on.

The tense watchers on the crest saw the horses rear and slew around before the onslaught, cramping the front wheels. Over went the stage, its crash rising above the tumult. The traces snapped and the horses tore off through the brush, bowling over cows in their way. The driver and the guard soared through the air to land at the edge of the brush, dimly seen through the rising dust cloud. The herd split, flowed on either side of the wreck and went careening around the bend to the north.

'Lord! What a mess!' Weston exclaimed. 'I'm afraid the driver and guard are killed or badly hurt. We'll get down there and see what we can do to help. We — blazes!'

Around the bend had bulged the pursuing horsemen. Flashes of orange flame gushed from their ranks. The reports flung back a thousand echoes.

'It's a hold-up!' Weston shouted. 'They stampeded the cows into the stage on purpose.'

From the brush that flanked the trail on the left, fire spurted. A rider reeled in his saddle. Yells of rage arose. Rifles boomed, smoke billowed. Again a spurt of fire from the brush. The guard or the driver was still alive and giving a good account of himself.

Weston swung from the saddle, sliding his Winchester from the boot in the same movement.

'Unfork!' he called to Leah. 'Down! Down on the ground.'

He dropped to one knee as he spoke, the rifle clamped to his shoulder. The muzzle spurted smoke. Answering the report, a man spun from his saddle. Weston shifted the rifle muzzle the merest trifle and fired again.

A second horseman went down. The others whirled and sent a storm of lead up the slope in the direction of their unseen attacker.

'Down!' Weston shouted to Leah in an

agony of apprehension as bullets clipped the leaves over his head. 'Hug the ground!' He fired a third time and saw one of the outlaws slump forward, gripping the horn for support. Answering slugs came closer. The raiders couldn't see him, but they could see the smoke from his gun; they were getting the range.

Weston pulled trigger a fourth time. A horse began to buck and leap. From the brush to the left of the trail swirled smoke. Another horse apparently went crazy. Weston took careful aim.

As at a word of command, the outlaws whirled their mounts and went racing back the way they had come, two riderless horses pounding after their follows. Weston emptied the magazine after them but did not score a hit as far as he could see. Another instant and they were out of sight. He shoved fresh cartridges into the magazine and stood up.

'Come on,' he told Leah, 'We'll get down there now and see what we can do.'

They sent their mounts charging down the slope. Weston raised his voice as they neared the trail.

'Hold your fire,' he called. 'We're coming to help you.'

'I'm holding it!' a voice replied hoarsely.

Crashing through a final fringe of brush, they jerked their horses to a slithering halt on the trail. From behind a boulder on the far side of the track the shoulders and ashen face of the guard rose into view.

'Feller,' he panted, 'you sure saved my bacon, and Hank's, too, if he ain't dead already. Scared the fall busted his neck.'

'What were they after?' Weston asked as he swung to the ground.

'Nigh on to thirty thousand dollars in the strongbox, payroll and supplies money for the quicksilver mines. They'd have got it if it wasn't for you.'

'Come on out,' Weston told him. 'Everything's under control, for the time being, anyhow.'

'Can't,' the guard gasped, his face twisting. 'Leg busted. Can't move.'

Weston started across the trail to him, then abruptly halted, staring at the two dead men lying face up in the trail. He uttered a sharp exclamation.

'What is it, Jim?' Leah asked.

'This one, the little one with the crooked nose,' Weston replied in a strained voice. 'He was one of the three I had the row with in the Orville saloon up in New Mexico.

'So it *was* a bunch from down here!' he muttered. Shaking his head, he strode across to where the injured guard was propped against the sheltering boulder, his face working with pain. Nearby lay the driver, very still but breathing.

Weston's keen mind took in the situation instantly. He turned to the girl.

'Leah,' he said, 'head up the trail. A quarter of a mile farther on you should find an easy place to climb the sag. Hightail to the holding spot. You can find your way?'

'Yes, I can find my way,' she replied.

'Get Peters and Hardy and a bunch of the boys and tell them to hustle down here,' Weston resumed. 'Tell them not to spare their horses. I'll need help with the guard and driver. No, not up the slope here. Hard going. You'll do better on around the bend.'

The girl gave him a searching look, but she only said, 'All right, Jim.'

'And, Leah ——'

'Yes, Jim?'

'Ride fast!'

'I will.' She sent Rambler racing forward and an instant later vanished around the bend.

'I don't think I fooled her,' Weston muttered.

'Fooled her?' echoed the guard.

'Yes, I believe she knows what's in the wind. Listen, those devils will come back once they get over their scare and realise there was only one man shooting at them from up top the sag. They won't let thirty thousand dollars slip through their fingers if they can help it. Won't be long, either. And they'd do for you and the driver. We've got to try and hold them off till help arrives. I sent her around by the trail on the chance they might see her top the sag if she went up the slope here. Let me do what I can for that leg of yours.'

Whipping out his knife, he slit the guard's corduroy britches above the site of the injury.

'Not compounded, anyhow, thank the Lord!' he muttered. 'Stay right in that position, now.'

Working with swift efficiency, he cut a couple of stout branches from the growth, shaved one side of each and used them to splint the broken bone, securing them in place with his tie rope. The guard groaned and swore, but endured the torment, sweat beading his face.

Once the splints were in place, the pain eased somewhat. He rolled a cigarette with shaking fingers, shooting glances southward along the trail.

Weston picked up the unconscious driver, cradling him easily in his arms. He called to

Ashes and, with the big moros pacing behind him, carried the driver some distance into the brush on the far side of the trail. He deposited him gently on the fallen leaves, felt of his heart, which was beating slowly but steadily, and listened a moment to his stentorous breathing.

'Pretty bad hurt, maybe a skull fracture, but maybe he's got a chance to pull through,' he told Ashes. 'Anyhow, I don't think there's much chance of him coming to soon. You and he ought to be fairly safe here, I hope. Stay put now, horse.' He dropped the split reins to the ground, knowing that was all needed to hold Ashes, and returned to the guard who, puffing hard on his cigarette, looked somewhat better.

'You really think those sons will come back?' he asked.

'Yes, I do,' Weston replied. 'It won't take them long to figure that one horse can't pack three men, plus better than a hundred pounds in gold and silver, even if they don't know one is crippled and another knocked out. They'll know the stage horses are gone. So in my opinion they'll figure we'll stay right here, or at least two will, to guard the money, even should the third ride off for help. Yes, I think they'll come back just as soon as it gets a little darker, but not dark enough for us to slip away and hide under cover of it, taking the strongbox with us. Of course I may be wrong in all this — hope I am — but I don't think so.'

'You figure they won't know the girl was with you and rode to get help?'

'Unlikely, I'd say,' Weston replied. 'As I said, it wouldn't take them long to figure that only one man was shooting from the crest, which would lead them to believe he was alone. Well, anyhow, all we can do is sit tight and hope my boys will get here in time to do some good. Back of these rocks is as good a place as any, I guess.'

'How about the money?'

'Leave it where it is. We can't be bothered with it, even if it was safe to try and get it out of the overturned coach. If they get us they'll get it. If they don't, they won't. How you feeling?'

'Better,' said the guard. 'Think I can risk another cigarette?'

'Take a chance on it,' Weston answered. 'I don't figure they'll show for a little while yet. Still rather light, but getting shadowy fast.'

The guard rolled his brain tablet and puffed gratefully, covering the tiny glow with his hand. Weston crouched comfortably behind the big boulder, his eyes fixed on the bend in the trail, his ears listening for sounds from any direction. He calculated how long it would take Leah to reach the holding spot and Price and the boys to arrive. The conclusions were not too encouraging.

The anxious, nerve-tightening minutes dragged past. Then he tensed at the guard's low whisper:

'I think I hear something.'

Chapter XII

Weston heard it too, the soft plopping of slow hoofs in the dust of the trail. He raised his rifle, got a good rest on the uneven edge of the boulder and waited.

Around the bend drifted a single horseman, peering with out-thrust neck. He halted his mount and swept the overturned coach and its environs with eyes that gleamed in the shadow of his hat-brim.

Weston lined sights with his breast. Then he shifted the rifle muzzle the merest trifle; it was a bit too much like cold-blooded murder. Even as the fellow straightened, half-turned as if to call to others, Weston squeezed the trigger.

The report rang out like a thunderclap in the silence. The rider gave a shrill yelp and swayed back in the saddle, clutching at his blood-spurting shoulder. With another yell he whirled his horse and flashed back around the bed, from which came a chorus of shouts and curses. Weston sent a second slug whining after him, then plucked two cartridges from his belt and shoved them into the magazine.

'May need every shot,' he muttered to the guard. 'Got your gun ready? I figure the ball's about due to open. That was just the overture.'

'The over-what?' sputtered the guard. 'No matter; I'm all set. Let 'em come!'

They came with a rush, yelling and shooting. Bullets thudded into the overturned coach. Then the outlaws realised their mistake and sent slugs whistling toward where the quarry really was holed up, firing at the flashes of the two rifles spitting death at them from behind the boulder. Leaves showered down, splinters of rock flew through the air, bullets ricocheted with angry whines.

Weston and the guard fired as fast as they could pull trigger, shooting at the elusive shadows ducking and weaving amid the shadows. It was fast and furious work, with no time really to take aim.

The outlaws gave way, sweeping around the bend and out of sight. Two more of their number lay motionless in the dust.

'They got a bellyful!' exulted the guard.

'Maybe, but I'm afraid not,' Weston replied

as he reloaded. 'Now I figure our real trouble is going to start. They'll very likely circle through the chaparral and try to surround us. Thank Pete it's getting darker under this brush. That'll help some.

'See?' he whispered a few minutes later as a slug whined past from an angle. 'Here, let me help you flatten out on the ground. Hug the dirt as close as you can and shoot at a flash if you see one.'

He stretched out beside his companion, his rifle shoved to the front, and lay peering and listening, finger crooked on the trigger.

But there was nothing to shoot at, and more slugs fired at random whistled past. They were coming from three directions now as the outlaws slowly closed the circle. One creased the flesh of Weston's left shoulder. A second twitched his hat crown. Still a third chipped a bit of bark from one of the guard's leg splints, causing that worthy to curse fervently under his breath.

'They're getting the range,' Weston muttered. 'Things don't look so good. Keep your head down. Nothing to see, anyhow.'

From the distant ridge crest suddenly sounded a shouting, then a prodigious crashing of brush drawing swiftly nearer. The whole slope erupted with gunfire.

'Flatten out!' Weston barked to his companion. 'It's the boys, and they're letting off bullets in every direction. Blazes! I hope they don't squash the driver and do for my horse.'

Nearby sounded other crashings as the outlaws fled madly for their horses. A moment later the drumming of their frenzied flight faded into the distance.

The Lucky Seven cowboys, fighting the brush in the near-dark, were howling curses. Tom Peters' stentorian bellow rose above the din ——

'We're coming, Jim! Hold 'em, feller, hold 'em!'

'Stop shooting!' Weston roared. 'You'll kill *us!*'

Peters' thundering voice relayed the order. The gunfire ceased. The yells and crashings redoubled. Peters' foam-flecked horse burst through the final fringe and skated on the trail.

'Where are they?' the big cowboy boomed. 'Let me at 'em. You all right, Jim?'

'Fine as frog hair,' Weston replied, rising to his feet. 'But you sure got here just in time. Things were getting sort of warm.'

Other punchers came charging into view, and more and more. 'There's about fifty still coming,' chuckled Peters. 'Guess the whole round-up force'll be here before we're

133

finished. Here's Miss Leah. Couldn't stop her from coming along.'

Weston shook his head. 'Guess nobody can stop her from doing what she's a mind to,' he said. 'But if it wasn't for her, I guess we'd have been goners. Much obliged, Leah, for saving some worthless carcasses.'

The red-haired girl essayed a smile, but even in the dusk Weston could see her lips tremble. He reached up and swung her down from the saddle.

'You've been too long in the hull,' he said. 'Walk around a bit and you'll feel better.'

'Peters,' he called, 'there's sotol growing in the brush along the trail. Break off some dry stalks for torches. Get one going quick and come with me. A badly hurt man in the brush over there. And the guard here has a broken leg. We'll pack them to the holding spot — that's a lot closer than town — and put them to bed in the wagons while somebody hightails for the doctor and the sheriff.'

More and more of the round-up crew kept arriving, until the trail around the wrecked coach was crowded and aglare with burning sotol. Two stretchers were improvised from poles and coats and lashed between steady-pacing horses. The injured men were placed in them and at once headed for the holding spot. The driver regained consciousness before the operation was completed and cursed all and sundry and the day he was born. Weston decided he wasn't very seriously hurt but that it was best he should be kept quiet until the doctor looked him over. A searching party located the stage horses, tangled in a thicket, and freed them from the broken harness. The bodies of the four slain outlaws were left lying where they fell until the sheriff could examine them.

Mindful of the advice of Cromwell, the Indian agent, Weston turned out their pockets but discovered nothing of interest save a rather large sum of money. He dropped the coins in a heap beside the bodies, grinned and turned his back. When he looked that way again, the ground was bare.

'Guess the county treasury can get along without it, and the boys can use it,' he observed to Leah. 'Well, this has been a day! And a heck of a way to run a round-up.'

The strongbox was hauled from the overturned stage, the lock blasted off by a forty-five slug and the contents stowed in Weston's and Peters' saddle-pouches.

'Well, guess that takes care of everything,' Weston said. 'Let's get home; I'm hungry.'

He paused long enough to take another long took at the scrawny outlaw with the crooked nose.

'Yes, he was one of the three that tried to kill me in New Mexico,' he repeated. 'This is getting darned interesting.'

'And dangerous, I'm afraid,' Leah replied. 'Dangerous for you. Do you think they'll try again?'

Weston shrugged. 'Possibly,' he conceded, 'but I don't propose to bother my head about it. And,' he added, his eyes suddenly cold, 'I'm pretty well convinced now it's the same bunch that did for your brother. Well, we appear to be evening up the score a bit. This makes sixteen altogether, I believe, but still some more to go.'

Leah shuddered. 'It's terrible,' she murmured. 'I love this land, but it *is* a terrible country.'

'Want to pull out?' he asked playfully.

Her chin went up. 'No, I don't, and I don't intend to,' she retorted. 'Let's go.'

No trace of the slain outlaws' horses was found by the cowboys who scoured the brush in quest of them.

'Followed the others,' Sam Hardy concluded. 'Looks like maybe they were trained to do just that.'

'Quite likely,' Weston conceded. 'Let's go,' he repeated to Leah.

They climbed the slope in silence and were topping the crest when Leah spoke.

'Jim,' she asked, 'how many were in the bunch that murdered my brother?'

'About a dozen,' Weston replied.

'And sixteen have been killed?'

'That's about right.'

'Then it looks like ——'

Weston laughed mirthlessly. 'But it isn't like it looks like,' he interrupted. 'There might have been quite a few more who didn't take part in that particular raid.'

'For goodness sakes! How many could there be in such a band?' she asked.

'Hard to tell,' Weston answered. 'Curly Bill Brocius over in Arizona could call up a hundred if he needed them, and Kingfisher in east Texas almost as many. Some of those organisations are mighty big. Besides, it's pretty certain that the hellion who heads the outfit is still running around loose, and that kind of a head grows a new body mighty fast. An owlhoot leader of his proven ability doesn't have any trouble recruiting replacements for his losses. Plenty of suitable material between here and the Border. You have to squash the head to kill the snake, and the head is still plenty lively, not much doubt as to that.'

'I wonder who it is?'

'That's a question,' Weston replied. 'Maybe somebody right here in this section, and folks will be almighty surprised when and if he is uncovered. Then again, the head of the outfit may direct operations from down around the Mexican Border. That's happened. Could have men planted in some of the spread outfits, or in town, who tip him off to likely possibilities. Somebody seems to know things that aren't supposed to be generally known. The guard told me that the stage carrying that money shipment was supposed to be a secret. Wasn't supposed to be shipped for several days. But somebody either learned about it or caught on some way. Nobody was supposed to know the cows that were stolen the day your brother was killed were holed up in a certain canyon, but somebody knew. Has happened a number of times. Oh, it's no brush-popping bunch of makeshift raiders. It's a well-organised outfit of hardened criminals with a mighty smart devil directing operations. Sort of like the bunch that operated around Tombstone, Arizona, or over around San Antonio.'

'And their business is robbery and murder,' Leah commented.

'That's about right.'

'And it's likely they won't feel exactly friendly toward you for frustrating the attempted robbery today?'

Weston shrugged again. 'All in the day's work,' he said. 'I don't care for their friendship, anyhow.'

'But meanwhile you are in danger.'

'When your number's up, it's up,' he replied cheerfully. 'If it isn't up, nobody can put it up.'

'A comforting philosophy but, I fear, somewhat casuistic,' she observed dryly.

Weston laughed and did not argue the point.

They rode on through the hushed dark.

Jim Weston didn't go to sleep that night but waited for the doctor, who arrived shortly after midnight. He gave scant heed to the stage driver, who was sitting up smoking and drinking coffee.

'Skull like a cannon ball,' he told Weston. 'No fracture and no signs of concussion. That head of his would turn a rifle bullet. But the guard will be laid up for a few weeks. You did a good job of splintering that leg. Otherwise he might have suffered a compound fracture. I'll send a wagon for him tomorrow. The other old coot can ride in, or walk. Neither would do him any damage. A representative for the stage company will be out tomorrow; he'll want to talk to you. So will the sheriff when he shows up, I reckon.'

'I'm leaving the money in the chuck wagon with Dirty Shirt to keep an eye on it,' Weston said. 'If they want to talk to me, they'll find me out on the range. Miss Carol can tell them what happened.'

'She's been having quite a time of it since she landed here,' chuckled the doctor. 'Wouldn't be surprised if she's getting fed up with this wild and woolly section.'

'She isn't,' Weston replied. The old doctor shot him a shrewd glance, and chuckled again.

In the dark hour before the dawn, a wrathful meeting was in progress in an old cabin back of the north-eastern hills. There were eleven hard-looking characters present, one with a bandaged shoulder and his arm in a sling. A tall man muffled in a long coat, his hat pulled low over his eyes, sat at the head of a table with his back to the light.

'That infernal Weston!' he was saying. 'Three times now he's beat us out of a good haul. That hombre's got to go.'

'How?' somebody asked.

'We'll figure a way,' said the tall man.

'A couple of us might pick a fight with him in a Marta saloon and make it look like self-defence,' a voice suggested.

'Yes? That was tried up in New Mexico. Gulden got himself killed and Slinky was drilled through the shoulder, and Weston got away with a scratch. The hellion is poison with a gun. It's got to be something subtle and well planned. Leave it to me to figure out something that will work.'

'How about the girl?' asked another voice.

'I'll take care of her personally.'

'That's a risky business,' one of the men lounging by the glowing stove objected. 'Lay a hand on a woman in this country and you'll have the whole state after you, including the Rangers. Mighty risky.'

'The way I'll handle it there'll be no risk,' replied the tall man. 'But Weston has got to go. We're playing for big stakes that will eventually put us all on Easy Street. We can't afford to have our twine tangled by a nosy cowhand.'

'Everything's been breaking wrong of late,' grumbled another. 'We're getting pretty well thinned out.'

'The less to share. And what we've lost have been mostly new men. Saves us the bother of getting rid of them later.'

Chuckles greeted the callous remark.

The tall man stood up, his face still in the shadow. 'I'm riding,' he announced. 'You fellows take it easy for a few days. I'll have something good lined up soon. And try to think about what I told you. *Weston has got to go!'*

Chapter XIII

After less than four hours sleep, Jim Weston was out on the range at dawn. Leah remained at the chuck wagon to await the arrival of the sheriff and the representative of the stage company. Old Dirty-Shirt had hidden the gold and silver in the 'coonie', the bagged-down rawhide stretched to the running gear under the wagon and used to store firewood.

'Hope I don't forget and chuck it on the fire,' he said to Leah. 'They oughta hand Jim a hefty helpin' of it for what he did.'

'I'm afraid he wouldn't accept it,' Leah replied. 'He has notions concerning such matters.'

'Uh-huh, he has notions,' Dirty said. 'Sometimes I think he has too darned many notions. What Jim needs is a woman to look after. If he had a woman to look after and pervide for, he might forget some of his finicky notions.'

'Doubtless he would,' Leah agreed gravely, but with a dimple peeping at the corner of her red mouth.

'Ain't right for a young feller to be amblin' around loose all the time like a maverick,' said Dirty. 'Liable to get into trouble and all sorts of things.'

'Quite likely,' agreed Leah.

'Well, ma'am, why don't *you* try to do something about it?' suggested Dirty.

'Perhaps I will,' Leah said very gravely. 'Perhaps I can find him a nice girl to look after. I know one in Chicago who would do fine. She used to be my room mate, and her name is Rose.'

She was gone before old Dirty could frame an adequate reply.

The sheriff arrived shortly before noon, accompanied by three deputies, the stage company's representative and four pack mules. He listened attentively to Leah's account and nodded his approbation.

'A fine chore,' he said. 'Coudn't have been better.' The company's representative echoed his sentiments.

'My company is greatly indebted to Mr. Weston,' he said. 'He will receive a letter that will more adequately express its gratitude. Please induce him to regard it in a sensible manner, Miss Carol.'

Old Dirty winked at Leah, who blushed in spite of herself.

'I'll go down and pick up those carcasses,' added the sheriff. 'I figure to pack 'em to town and lay 'em out for folks to look over. Maybe somebody will recognise 'em and give me a chance to run down the ones that got away. Trout,' he said to the company man, 'we'll shove the money into our saddle pouches and take it along with us. I aim to head back to town by way of the Terlingua Trail; it's shorter.'

Leah had gone for a ride late in the afternoon when she saw a horseman approaching from the north. A few minutes later she recognised Nelson Haynes.

'Why, hello, Miss Carol,' he called. 'May I join you?'

'If you wish,' she acceded.

'I do wish,' he smiled, and reined his horse alongside Rambler.

'Hear you had some excitement down this way yesterday evening,' he observed. 'I remained at my ranch-house yesterday and missed it.'

'I had rather more of it than I liked,' she replied. 'I would prefer no more such experiences.'

'Such things happen in this country,' Haynes said lightly. 'Elsewhere, too, for that matter. Seems I've read of considerable excitement in your Chicago at times.'

Leah laughed and did not deny the truth of the statement.

They paced their horses westward across the prairie and paused on the bank of the creek that flowed down across Haynes' spread. The sun was setting and shooting red rays across the hurrying water.

'The life blood of the rangeland,' Haynes remarked.

'It looks like blood in that light,' Leah commented.

'Yes, and the time may come when it's tinged with blood,' said Haynes. 'Water is vital to dry country, but it is also sometimes provocative of trouble. The first range war of which we have any record was fought over water.'

'Yes?' the girl replied questioningly.

'Yes. You'll find the account in the Bible, Book of *Genesis* — "And Isaac's servants digged in the valley, and found there a well of springing water. And the herdmen of Gerar did strive with Isaac's herdmen, saying, 'The water is ours.' " Interesting, don't you think?'

'You appear to be widely read, Mr. Haynes,' she said.

'Rather, I have a retentive memory and

recall what I *have* read,' he corrected smilingly.

'Hello! here comes somebody. Why, it's Jim Weston.' He raised his voice in a shout of greeting. Weston, riding up from the south, turned his horse slightly to join them.

Haynes stayed for supper with the Lucky Seven outfit and, incidentally, monopolised Leah's company during the evening, and proved more than usually charming and entertaining. To his own intense irritation, Jim Weston found himself feeling awkward and constrained in contrast, and envying Haynes' debonair self-assurance. After a while, he excused himself on the pretext of checking on the night hawks who were circling the herd and soothing the cattle with song, or what passed for it. When he returned to the camp, Haynes had taken his departure. Leah was sitting by herself gazing broodingly into the fire. Abruptly she spoke.

'Jim,' she said, 'can you spare time in the morning to ride down to the south end of our ranch with me?'

'Of course,' Weston replied. 'But why do you keep saying *"our"* ranch? You're the sole owner.'

She smiled fleetingly. 'Perhaps because you always show such an interest in the place, as if it were your own,' she said.

'A man should have his employer's interests at heart,' he retorted, a note of irritation creeping into his voice.

'Yes, I suppose that's it; that would be your nature,' she conceded. 'Good night, Jim.' She walked to the chuck wagon and climbed into it. Weston sat on beside the fire.

Tom Peters sidled up to him, squatted on his heels and rolled a cigarette.

'That jigger, Haynes,' he remarked, 'seems to have a way with women.'

'Very likely,' Weston growled.

'And,' continued Peters, 'I've a notion he's getting sort of sweet on her.'

'Her?'

'You know who I mean,' growled Peters. 'Miss Leah.'

'Not beyond the realm of possibility,' Weston conceded.

'And it looks like we might be looking for a job, after all. I'm darned if I'd want to work for Haynes.'

'Why?' Weston asked irrelevantly.

'Darned if I know,' Peters admitted, 'but I wouldn't.'

'Well, I don't see as there is anything we can do about it,' said Weston.

Peters crushed his cigarette between vicious fingers and stood up.

'Jim,' he said disgustedly, 'you're a fool!' and stalked off.

Weston gazed after him. 'Chances are I am,' he remarked to the fire, 'but I don't propose to make a bigger one of myself.'

CHAPTER XIV

The round-up was over. The shipping herds were rolling to the railroad and the loading pens, the cowboys getting ready for a celebration in town. The owners were well satisfied with the way the chore had been handled and complimented Jim Weston.

'Best darn cowman in Texas!' was the verdict.

Old Sam Hardy was *not* satisfied with the Lucky Seven tally. 'We've lost even more than I figured,' he declared. 'Jim, I tell you the sons-of-mothers are bleedin' us. We've got to do something about it.'

'Yes, but what?' Weston replied. 'I'll have to think this over a bit.'

That evening a hand brought the mail from town. One official-looking envelope was addressed to Jim Weston. He tore it open and extracted a short letter and a cheque for five hundred dollars, signed by an official of the stage company.

He read the letter and deliberately started to tear the cheque in two. But a quick little hand shot out and deftly relieved him of it before he could accomplish his purpose.

'No, you don't,' Leah said. 'You saved those people thirty thousand dollars and risked your life to do it. Look what the letter says, that they're sending this cheque as a small token of their appreciation and will be grateful to you if you will accept it in that spirit. You're going to accept it and put it in the bank. Promise me!'

'Oh, all right,' he replied sheepishly. 'I never can win an argument with you, but I don't particularly hanker for blood money.'

'It isn't blood money!' she denied indignantly. 'They're not trying to pay you for killing those outlaws, although somebody should. They're just trying to show their appreciation for what you did for them in saving them all that money. You're silly.'

'I guess maybe I am, in more ways than one,' he sighed.

The dimple showed as she returned the cheque. 'Anyhow, the fact that you are willing to admit it is refreshing,' she said.

Jim Weston considered what Sam Hardy had told him concerning the missing cattle. As a result, the Lucky Seven holding was patrolled day and night, especially the more northerly pastures. Men were also stationed in Clear Water Canyon to intercept anything that might attempt to go through, but with negative results.

'But we're still losin' 'em,' old Sam insisted wrathfully a few days later. 'Last night the rustlers got forty or fifty head off the new pasture where you drilled the wells. The cows have been drifting on to that ground, and I've been keeping a check on 'em. Not that I figured they'd be in any danger there. From there they'd have to head for Clear Water or cut back all the way south to the desert and then turn east. Which they sure couldn't do without being spotted by the jiggers ridin' line. But yesterday there were cows on that pasture that ain't there today.'

'Perhaps they drifted back off the pasture,' Weston suggested.

'You know darn well they didn't,' Hardy snorted. 'They wouldn't drift back off that good grass till they'd eaten the pasture over. You know that as well as I do. They were helped off, and that's all there is to it. I figure they *must* have gone through Clear Water Canyon. There must be a way they can slide 'em through without being spotted. Anyhow, they're gone.'

Weston didn't argue the point. He knew the old cowboy had an almost uncanny knack for spotting and remembering stock. If Hardy said the cows had been on that pasture one day and not the next, he was right.

Nelson Haynes dropped in one evening for a chat, and Leah and Weston discussed the problem with him.

'Ive been losing stock, too,' the Bar H owner declared angrily. 'And plenty, especially from my north pastures. I'm more vulnerable than you are here. Plenty of cracks up there they can shove them through, and we can't watch everything. Tell you what I think I'll do. I think I'll post some of my boys down on my south-east pasture, where they can keep an eye on the mouth of Clear Water Canyon. It's pretty well brush-grown and with lots of chimney rocks and ledges. They may have figured an undercover route.'

'Yes, it's possible,' Weston conceded, 'but unlikely. Still, as you say, it might be done.'

'Anyhow, I think I'll set a watch there,' said Haynes. 'May ride down there myself tomorrow night. If so, I'll see you in the morning.'

The following day Jim Weston, while puzzling over the aggravating situation, suddenly had a hunch. In consequence, he reshuffled his plans and did not ride to the canyon that night to help stand guard. Instead, shortly after dark he rode due south, accompanied by Peters, Hardy and three more hands. With them they took two laden pack mules.

They rode steadily until they reached the edge of the desert. Then they turned sharply east. Following the torturous Tornaga Trail, which flowed along the base of the Tornaga Hills, they reached Tornaga Pass where Arch Carol had met his death. Through the notch, the only possible southward route through the hills, they rode steadily until the pass began to narrow. Another mile and they drew rein. Searching about in the moonlight, they discovered a spot on the east slope where they could lie hidden but view the floor of the pass. Here they unloaded the supplies packed by the mules and made camp. Then they settled down comfortably to wait.

'Jim, this was sure a notion, all right,' chuckled Peters. 'The hellions will have to drive through this gap to head for the Border. And if they come this way, we've got 'em.'

'Yes,' agreed Weston. 'I wonder why we didn't think of it before, especially as we did trail the devils this way the day poor Arch was killed. Concentrating too hard on our immediate surroundings, I guess.'

The hours dragged slowly past. The great clock in the sky wheeled westward. The stars paled from gold to silver, dwindled to needle points of flame and vanished. In the east a pale glow of pearly rose deepened to scarlet, to gold. Somewhere a bird sang a liquid note. A little breeze shook down a myriad dew gems from the fading grass heads. The sun rose with a flashing of ten million spears, and it was day.

The drowsy cowboys yawned and straightened their cramped limbs. The horses whickered softly and cropped grass, eyeing the mules suspiciously.

'Well, you could hardly expect anything to happen last night,' observed Peters as he and Hardy busied themselves preparing something to eat. 'Not after they raided the night before, as Sam says they did. Chances are they'll pull something tonight. Hope so.'

'We'll sleep awhile after we've eaten,' Weston said, 'and be all set for another night of it. We've got enough chuck to last for several days, and I figure that sooner or later something will come this way.'

In the full light, Weston took stock of their surroundings. The camp was on the crest of a ledge of rock, in a little clearing only a few yards in diameter and fairly well brush-grown on three sides. Above was an almost barren stretch for thirty yards or so, ending against a second low and somewhat sloping ledge surmounted by a thick bristle of chaparral.

Thinking that perhaps the upper ledge would be better for the ambush, Weston climbed the slope and scrambled up the slanting rock. As he reached the crest, there was an angry squeal and a javelina pig, a sow with swollen dugs, scuttled out of sight at his feet. Evidently the critter had a nest of young in the thicket.

'Take it easy, old lady,' he laughed. 'I won't bother your babies.'

A glance around convinced him that the crest of the lower ledge was a more suitable site, so he slid back down the slope and returned to the camp.

After eating, the cowboys spread their blankets and slept till late afternoon. After that they cooked and ate another meal and lolled about smoking and chatting.

The gold of the afternoon faded to the silver-blue of dusk, deepened to purple. A great hush fell over the wild hill country. The dark closed down with gentle insistence, and the lonely vigil of the night began again.

Weston sat a litle apart, thinking.

The night passed without incident. The world awoke to song and gladness as a myriad little feathered choristers sang their paean of praise. The weary cowboys stretched, yawned, began preparations for breakfast.

'Looks like we're following a cold trail,' observed Sam Hardy.

'Maybe,' Weston conceded, 'but we'll give it another night. We —'

His voice trailed off as a sound drifted from down the pass, the thin bleat of a tired and disgusted steer. The cowboys tensed to hair-trigger alertness.

'By God, here they come!' exclaimed Peters, staring in the direction of the sound. 'Get set, boys!' All eyes were riveted on the pass below.

It was Weston's habitual watchfulness, plus an angry squeal by the javelina and the scutter of its hoofs, that saved them. Weston whirled to glance up the slope. His eyes caught a gleam as of sunlight on shifted metal.

'Take cover!' he yelled. 'Run!'

The cowboys dived right and left into the brush, a storm of lead speeding them on their way. One gave a retching cough, fell forward on his face and lay still. The others, muttering curses, crouched behind the ledge, staring at the smoke-spurting thicket above.

'Let them have it!' roared Weston. 'We'll be caught in a crossfire in another minute.'

A bellow of gunfire echoed the command as the punchers poured bullets into the growth that topped the upper ledge.

The advantage was theirs, for the moment. They had a rocky wall to shelter them, while the drygulchers had to rely on the concealing growth, and twigs and leaves don't offer much resistance to forty-five slugs. A howl of pain and a torrent of curses answered their fire; there were more yells as they continued to blast the thicket with lead, then a crackling and crashing as the attackers beat a hurried retreat.

But the fight wasn't won, not by a long shot. Into view on the pass floor bulged a dozen galloping steers. Behind them rode five men. Smoke spurted from their ranks. Peters cursed violently as a slug furrowed his leg. Jeth Bass reeled back, blood pouring down the side of his face. He rumbled an oath and flung his rifle to his shoulder. Weston was already shooting at the approaching riders.

'Keep peppering that brush up there, Sam,' he snapped to Hardy, without turning his head. 'If the others come back we're done. Ha! There's one of the hellions down. Good work, Jeth; it was you got him.'

'There goes another!' whooped Bass. 'Two down, three to go! Give 'em what for!'

But the three remaining riders apparently realised they had been left to fight the battle alone. They whirled their mounts and streaked back down the pass, bullets speeding them on their way. The two riderless horses galloped after them.

'Got a bellyful, eh?' chuckled Bass, wiping the blood from his gashed cheek.

'Careful,' Weston warned. 'Be sure those up above didn't stop before you show yourself. I don't think they did, but they might have. Send a couple more slugs up there, Sam. Aim high.'

Hardy did so. Weston motioned him to desist after the second shot. He raised his head cautiously and peered over the lip of the ledge, sweeping the thicket above with his keen gaze. Nothing moved there. He observed a bird that had been circling above the growth settle into it.

'Guess they've gone, all right,' he said. He levered himself over the ledge and went zigzagging up the slope, gun ready for instant action.

Nothing happened. He surmounted the second ledge and crouched in the brush, peering and listening.

There was no movement. He heard the javelina grunt nearby, and that was all. Still moving with care, he searched the growth. A little way back from the ledge he came upon a body sprawled in the brush. Examination showed the man had caught one squarely between the eyes. Weston continued his search but discovered nothing more except some blood spots leading up the slope. He retraced his steps to the ledge and called to his companions:

'Got one up here. Come and take a look at him.'

The hands did so. Nobody could recall ever seeing the dead man before, nor did anyone recognise the two bodies on the floor of the pass.

'Ornery-looking specimens,' growled Hardy. 'Well, we got three and they got one. Poor Russell, he was worth a hundred of this sort of scum. What will we do now, Jim?'

Weston glanced up the slope. 'Another one was winged.' he said, 'but I figure he kept on going. Those cows wouldn't have run far once they weren't being pushed. Round them up and see if they wear our brand.'

'Just what does it all mean?' asked Peters.

'Means we were outsmarted,' Weston

replied. 'We thought we were laying for them, but all the while they were laying for us. Caught on somehow to what we had in mind. Sent one bunch down the hillside beyond the pass to catch us from behind when the other bunch shoved the cows up the pass and held our attention.'

'If you hadn't been so quick to catch on, we'd have been goners,' Peters declared.

'Thank that old pig up there in the brush,' Weston replied. 'She cussed me out yesterday when I disturbed her. When I heard her squeal this morning I knew darn well something was prowling up there. Then I caught the flash of a gun-barrel and figured it was time to hunt cover.'

'Time to hunt cover was right,' grunted Peters. 'I felt the wind of several of those blue whistlers as I hit the ground. Here come the boys with the cows.'

As the small herd drew near, one of the hands raised his voice.

'They ain't ours,' he shouted. 'They're packing a Bar H burn.'

'Some of Haynes' cows, eh?' remarked Peters. 'Guess they must have slid 'em off one of his north pastures, or maybe he had 'em holed up somewhere. Maybe they caught on that everybody was watching Clear Water Canyon and decided to lay off our stuff for a while.'

'Not impossible,' Weston conceded. 'They only needed a few for bait, to draw our attention down the pass when we heard them bawl.'

'Connivin' cowards!' growled Peters. 'Now what, Jim?'

'We might as well head for home,' Weston replied. 'More news for the sheriff. Nothing we can do down here. Rope Russell's body to his horse. Wait till I give these hellions the onceover.'

Examination of the bodies turned up nothing of significance. As in former cases, there was a good supply of money.

'Take it and divide it up,' Weston told the hands. 'You've earned it.'

The order was obeyed with alacrity.

CHAPTER XV

The captured cattle made progress slow, and the day was drawing to a close when the weary cavalcade reached the Lucky Seven ranch-house. Leah cried a little as she gazed on Bob Russell's dead face.

'And he was so young, too,' she murmured. 'Jim, isn't it ever going to end?'

'I don't know,' Weston replied wearily. 'Not till we drop a loop on the hellion who's running things, I'm afraid. Come on to the house; we'll bury Bob tomorrow. Everything been going smoothly here?'

'Nothing has happened,' she replied. 'The boys watching the canyon had nothing to report. Mr. Haynes was here yesterday morning. When he didn't see you with the boys up at the canyon, he asked them why you weren't there and they told him what you had in mind. He rode down to verify it. He said if he had known what you intended to do, he would have gone along. Seemed disappointed that he didn't get the chance.'

'We could have used him,' Weston replied. 'Things were a bit warm for a while. Well, we got a few of his cows back for him, anyhow.'

When they reached the living-room, she pushed him into an easy-chair.

'You stay right there,' she ordered. 'You look thoroughly worn out. I'll get you some coffee. That ought to help.'

'Nice to have someone to wait on me,' he smiled. Her colour mounted a little as she replied, her voice very soft and low:

'And it's nice to have somebody to wait on.'

She was back shortly with the coffee, steaming hot. 'Drink this before you wash up and get ready to eat,' she said. 'You must be starved.'

'I am a mite lank,' he admitted. 'We didn't feel much like eating after the fight and headed for home without stopping to cook breakfast.'

Later, after they had eaten, they sat in the living-room and talked for a while. Finally silence fell between them. Weston smoked, while Leah sat gazing pensively into the fire. She spoke without turning her head.

'Jim, I have something to tell you,' she said.

'You have?'

'I have. Jim, yesterday morning Mr. Haynes asked me to marry him.'

'Yes?' Weston's lips were suddenly stiff.

'Yes, he did.'

'And what did you tell him?'

'I told him I wouldn't.'

'But why?' The question was out before he realised how it might be interpreted. In fact, his head was in such a whirl he hardly knew what he said.

Leah turned to face him. Her eyes were serious, but the dimple showed at the corner of her mouth.

'First and foremost, I don't love him. That, in my opinion, is reason enough. Secondly, I think he is much more interested in getting control of the Lucky Seven than in slipping a ring on my charming finger.'

Weston looked dazed. 'You sure he isn't in love with you?'

'Nelson Haynes is in love with nobody except Nelson Haynes, and I don't think he ever will be. What he's after is the Lucky Seven. He's willing to take on a wife he doesn't really want to get it.'

'But — but why?' Weston sputtered. 'It's a good spread, but that's all you can say for it. You'd think the hills were made of gold or silver instead of trap-rock and limestone.'

'The land to the south of our holding is gold and silver,' Leah replied.

'That desert!' scoffed Weston. 'There's no mineral down there; it's been gone over a hundred times.'

'There is potential gold down there, plenty of it,' Leah said. 'Oh, Jim, can't you understand? Can't you see that if he owned the Lucky Seven, Haynes would control the only real water in this section? You know and I know that the water of our creek could easily be diverted to flow due south instead of south-west, its present direction. If Haynes controlled the Lucky Seven, he could buy those millions of acres of state land for almost nothing. Then he could divert the creek to flow south. His creek also. He can't now, because our land blocks him. Those creeks are not navigable streams. Owning their sources, he could do whatever he pleased with the water. The arid land would become a garden and immensely valuable. Now do you understand?'

'Yes, I think I do,' Weston said. 'And I understand, too, why Arch Carol wouldn't sell to Haynes. He'd figured out what Haynes had in mind, and he knew that the ranches to the south-west would become worthless, and the people who owned them, his friends, would not only be ruined financially but would be driven from the homes they'd lived in all their lives and their fathers before them. It would have broken their hearts. Old-timers develop a great affection for their holdings, and nothing short of dynamite can pry them loose from the land that has become a part of them. So Arch Carol wouldn't sell, though at the time it would have been greatly to his personal advantage to do so. He was a man!'

Abruptly Weston stood up. He walked to the window and gazed blindly into the darkness, his eyes pale and cold, his lips twitching. For Jim Weston now understood what Leah did *not* understand yet. He whirled around to face her.

'Leah,' he said hoarsely, 'why didn't you tell me this before?'

'Because I didn't see any reason I should, knowing as I did that Nelson Haynes would never get the Lucky Seven,' she replied. 'Besides, I thought it would be fun to string him along a little. I figured it would be good for him! He's so darn sure of himself and unable to see how any woman could resist him. And, you know, there's a little of the cat in all women. We really get pleasure from playing with a man a bit as a cat plays with a mouse, especially when we know his affections aren't really involved and he can't be hurt seriously except in his vanity, which heals quickly. Perhaps there was a little pique involved, too. A woman doesn't like to think she stands second to a hunk of land.'

Although he was in no mood for mirth, Weston had to chuckle at this naïve feminine confession. But instantly his face became grim again.

'I'm going over to the bunk-house,' he said. 'I'll be back in a little while. Wait up for me.'

'I will,' she promised.

Weston walked slowly after he left the ranch-house, trying properly to evaluate what he had just learned. He paused at the bunk-house door a moment to marshal his badly scrambled faculties before lifting the latch and entering.

Some of the hands were playing cards, others were smoking and talking. Old Sam Hardy lay in his bunk reading. Weston called them to gather around him. In terse sentences he rehearsed what Leah had told him. The account was received with the silence of astonishment. Then Tom Peters gave a long whistle.

'So that's why the hellion was willing to offer about twice what the spread was worth at the time to get hold of it!' he exclaimed.

'And to do murder trying to get it,' observed Sam Hardy.

The others stared at the old cowboy. Then all eyes turned questioningly to Weston.

'Boy's, I'm afraid Sam's right,' the range boss said wearily. 'All the evidence certainly points that way. I see it all now — marvel of perspicacity,' he added with a bitter sarcasm directed at himself. 'Haynes is in a position to get wind of everything that goes on in the section. The other ranchers, although they disagree with him on many points, are comparatively friendly with him, and he has no difficulty learning from them what they have in mind. He learned about that herd in the canyon, the one we trailed into the Tornaga Pass where Arch Carol was killed. Of course he knew all about our drive to New Mexico, the route we planned to take, the fact that Cromwell, the agent, would have his men meet us at the New Mexico line. He had that fake telegram sent, telling Cromwell we would be delayed a week, so Cromwell's men wouldn't meet us. Then he sent his hellions on ahead of us to grab off the shipping herd if they got a chance, figuring the loss of all those cows would pretty well cripple the Lucky Seven. Added to our other losses because of him, it would have just about done it. Then he could have offered to buy the Lucky Seven when there wasn't anything much else for Miss Leah to do but sell, or he could have offered to lend her money, with the ranch as security, knowing that if he kept on running off our cows she couldn't meet the note when it fell due. I've a strong notion that if I'd ridden up to the canyon the other night as I originally planned to do, I'd have been killed. The trap he set for us down in the Pass was the real giveaway. Nobody but Haynes, aside from our own boys, knew we were down there. They told Haynes when he asked why I wasn't at the canyon. He rode down here, verified what they said, and sent his hellions to drygulch us. As I said, he's in a position to learn what goes on in the section, like the payroll money for the quicksilver mines. He's a stage company stockholder and owns stock in the Marta bank and is a director. Shrewd, salty, and merciless. Remember, he has been here only a couple of years, and it wasn't long after he bought in the section that the wide-looping and robbing really got going strong. Trace him back, and the chances are we'd find he's been mixed up in plenty elsewhere.'

'You figure his hands are in on it, too?' asked Jeth Bass.

'I'd say no,' Weston replied. 'At least they

170

never take part in the raids. Haynes is too smart to use his riders for the chore. If one were killed or captured and recognised, the jig would be up. In fact, I doubt they know anything of what's going on. He can keep them off the range when he runs wide-looped cattle north over his holdings. Running the cows that way, he has no trouble circling them through the hills and to the Tornaga Pass, with a straight path from there on to the Border and his connections down there. See how it stands? What do you think?'

'What do *I* think?' growled big Tom Peters, opening and shutting his great hands. 'I think you've made a plumb straight throw. Just wait till I get my squeezers on that snake-blooded, murderin' thief!'

A chorus of like remarks rose on all sides. Weston held up his hand to still the tumult.

'Hold it!' he warned. 'Remember, we haven't one iota of proof against Haynes; not a thing that would stand up in court. It won't do for us to tip our hand. If he suspects we've caught on, he'll cover up and we'll never drop a loop on him. And he's smart, smart as a barrel full of foxes. If you happen to run into him, any of you, don't act a bit different from the way you always have. This thing has got to be handled carefully if we're to get anywhere. Now that we're on to him, he won't have things so easy. We know who to watch, and if we play our cards right, we'll tangle his twine for him.'

'Do you figure to tell the sheriff?' asked Peters.

Weston shook his head. 'He'd either think we were loco or he would go asking Haynes questions, which is the last thing we want to have happen. We'll go it on our own. Perhaps we can set a trap for him. I'll think about it. Maybe if we give him enough rope he'll hang himself. Well, I'll be seeing you.'

'Where you going, Jim?' Peters asked.

'I'm going to the ranch-house,' Weston replied, 'to settle something with Miss Leah once and for all.'

After the door closed, Tom Peters turned complacently to his companions.

'Gents,' he said, 'we've got a home!'

When he arrived at the ranch-house, Weston found Leah sitting where he had left her. He wasted no time.

'Leah,' he said, 'you meant it when you said you didn't love Nelson Haynes and wouldn't marry him, didn't you?'

'Of course I meant it,' she answered.

'Then would — if — I — we ——'

'Oh, you poor helpless dear!' she interrupted. 'Of course I'll marry you, if that's what you're trying to ask. I made up my mind quite a while ago to do just that. I — Oh! Goodness gracious! You don't realise how strong you are! And, darling — I — really — have — to breathe — a little!'

Later, quite a while later, when they were occupying a chair big enough for one and strong enough for two, Weston repeated briefly what he had told the cowboys in the bunk-house. Leah's eyes darkened with horror as the tale unfolded.

'It doesn't seem possible!' she whispered when he ceased speaking. 'Jim, are you sure?'

'Yes,' Weston replied, 'I am sure.'

Leah drew a long shuddering breath. 'Jim, what are we going to do?'

'I don't know yet,' he admitted frankly. 'As I told the boys, try and set a trap for him, I suppose, or perhaps catch him red-handed in something, which won't be easy to do. He's smart. By the way, how did he take your refusal?'

'In a very pleasant and gentlemanly way. He laughed and said he could wait, that he didn't think I'd marry anyone else. Now what did he mean by that, I wonder?'

Weston's lips tightened. He had a very good idea what Nelson Haynes meant.

Haynes had proven himself a ruthless killer who would allow nothing to stand in his way. He decided not to tell Leah; no sense in worrying her. But as it happened, as her next words told him, Leah had already guessed what Nelson Haynes meant.

'Jim,' she said, her voice trembling a little, 'I'm afraid.'

'Nothing will bother you, honey,' he hastened to reassure her.

'I'm not afraid for myself, dear,' she said. 'I'm afraid, horribly afraid, for you.'

'Don't worry,' he comforted her. 'I can take care of myself.' He hastened to turn the conversation into more cheerful channels.

'So you made up your mind to marry me quite a while ago?' he teased.

'Jim,' she said, 'I'm going to marry you, but not for a while. And we mustn't breathe a word to a soul just yet.'

'Why?'

'Because if he doesn't know about it, I'm pretty sure Nelson Haynes will keep coming to see me. It will give me the creeps to have him around, but I'll stand it, for I think Nelson Haynes is the kind of creature that only a woman can hope to deal with successfully.'

'Perhaps you're right,' he conceded, but

dubiously. 'Maybe with you he'll tip his hand. Only I'm not so sure I want you to play such a game with him. He's deadly.'

'Repeating your own words, I can take care of myself. And remember —' once again the resemblance to Arch Carol, that tough old fighter, was startling — 'Nelson Haynes was responsible for the death of my brother. And he tried to kill you!'

Breakfast the following morning was more than usually hilarious. The cowboys were in a gay mood, and quips ran around the table in an endless string. Leah sat for the most part with downcast eyes, and when they raised to meet Jim Weston's, the colour in her cheeks deepened.

After the hands trooped out and she and Weston paused in the living-room for a few minutes, she said:

'Jim, I think the boys have caught on.'

'Wouldn't be surprised,' he agreed. 'But we don't have to worry; they'll keep a tight latigo on their jaws until we give the word to ease off. Well, I've got to go and lay out their chores for them. I discontinued the patrol last night. Figured the hellions would be too busy licking their wounds to pull anything. But we've got to be on the lookout for them now.'

'What did you do with Haynes' cattle you

brought back with you?' she asked.

'Turned them into the cow corral. I figure Haynes will come snooping around before long. We can tell him to send some of his hands down to pick them up. I prefer not to have any of our boys around his place at present. They're in a pretty ugly temper where he is concerned and might let something slip.'

'You riding the range today?'

Weston shook his head. 'I'll attend to some bookwork I've been putting off while I wait for the sheriff to show up; he should be here around noon, I'd say. I sent Blaine to town first thing to notify him of the latest trouble. He's got three more to add to his collection. The county will go broke paying funeral expenses. He'll lay them out for inspection, but the chances are he won't have any more luck than he did with the others. If anybody recognises them they don't admit it. Perhaps nobody in town really does. Haynes is too smart to allow his devils to hang around Marta. I'd say they do their drinking at Alpine or Marathon, or maybe even way up at Van Horn. Those pueblos are out of the county and our sheriff's jurisdiction.'

'I see,' Leah said thoughtfully. 'But where do they live when they're around here?'

'That's something I'd sure like to find out,' Weston replied grimly. 'I may take a whirl at trying.'

Chapter XVI

The sheriff arrived shortly before noon. 'You're keeping me busy, but you're sure thinning out the hellions these past few months,' he said to Weston.

'Yes, but we've lost five good men, including Arch Carol,' Weston replied bitterly.

'A bad business, a mighty bad business,' the sheriff said sadly. 'Poor old Arch was a right jigger. I'm doing all I can, Jim. I've rode the hills down to the south-east time and again, and so have my deputies, trying to get a line on the hellions or pick up some clue, but we haven't had any luck. Looks like you're the only one who can make any headway against the devils.'

'I've just been lucky in happening to run into them at the right time,' Weston replied deprecatingly.

'Here's hoping your luck holds out,' said the sheriff. 'But be careful; it's a bad bunch.'

After the sheriff departed with his deputies and his pack mules, Weston experienced certain qualms of uneasiness. He wondered if he had done right in not confiding what he knew, or rather what he suspected. He was not a peace officer and had had no training along such lines. He might well bungle the business or blunder into a trap. So far luck had been with him, but luck could change, and luck was not exactly the thing to depend on in such a hazardous undertaking.

He took some comfort from the fact that Sheriff Knolles was a former cowhand who had been appointed a deputy and then had been elected to office and had had no special training himself. Well, he had acted for the best and could only hope he hadn't made a mistake.

Two hours before midnight, Weston rode south. He took with him seven men, including Tom Peters and Jeth Bass. The others, with old Sam Hardy in charge, were left at the spread with instructions to keep an eye on things and a check on cattle that might prove tempting to the wide-loopers.

'If you see something, don't start a row,' Weston cautioned. 'You'd be outnumbered and would end up in bad trouble. Just keep watch and see if anything is missing. Sam knows every cow we've got by her first name, and I don't think they can lift anything without him catching on.

'As I said, I'm playing a hunch,' he exclaimed. 'I've been trying to put myself in Haynes' place and anticipate just what he will do. I believe he'll think we won't pay any attention to the Pass any more, concluding that he wouldn't take a chance on running a bunch through there again. I believe he'll figure that and *will* run a bunch through. Yes, it's just a hunch, but it might pay off. We're heading for the Pass, and we're going to stay there till we learn something or decide definitely that Haynes is going to lay off for a while.'

'It might work,' concluded Peters. 'Anyhow, I can't see that we have anything to lose by giving it a whirl. Many a pot is lost because a jigger overlooks his hand and misses a chance to fill it.'

Two pack mules loaded with provisions but not too heavily to prevent them from making good speed were taken along. Confident that their departure was not witnessed, the posse rode south.

Night brooded over the rangeland like a nesting bird. The stars were glowing grapes of light in a sky of black-purple velvet. A faint wind stirred the grass-heads and sent a ripple of dusty silver waving across the prairie. In the east a sullen bank of clouds climbed slowly over the jagged crests of the hills.

The miles flowed back under the churning irons. The posse turned eastward, climbed between the jaws of the pass and sped on until the site of the previous camp was reached. Once again the Lucky Seven punchers took up their vigil through the hours of darkness.

Hour after hour they watched and waited, and saw nothing save the lonely stars, and heard nothing but the whisper of the wind in the dark trees.

The dawn broke. The weary cowboys cooked some breakfast and rolled up in their blankets to sleep until late afternoon.

Weston slept but little. He was taking no chances, even though an approaching herd would advertise its presence long before it came in sight.

Another meal was cooked, and the watchers were partaking of it when Tom Peters abruptly raised his head in an attitude of listening.

'Something coming!' he exclaimed, dropping a hand to his gun-butt.

'One horse, coming fast,' said Weston. 'Get set, but don't go off half-cocked till we see who it is. Funny, somebody sashaying down here hell-bent-for-election.'

Louder and louder sounded the pounding of fast hoofs. A horseman bulged around the curve of the pass several hundred yards to the north. Weston peered with puckered lids.

'Blazes! It's Sam Hardy!' he exclaimed. 'Now what the devil ——'

He raised his voice in greeting.

Hardy waved his hand and a moment later sent his horse scrambling up the slope.

'Nothing happened?' he asked as he dismounted.

'Not a thing,' Weston replied.

'Well, there should have,' said old Sam. 'Last night the rustlers got something like two hundred head from the north-east pasture.'

Weston stared at him. 'You sure, Sam?'

'Of course I'm sure,' growled the old puncher. Weston's brows knit and for a moment he stood silent.

'Well,' he finally said, 'that must mean they picked them up late and couldn't make the pass before daylight. Evidently they holed them up somewhere for a while. They won't keep them there for long, however, wherever it is. Too risky. A herd that size penned up away from its customary feeding ground would raise a racket that could be heard for miles. Haynes is too smart to take such a chance a minute longer than he has to. They'll be along tonight, and we'll be all set for them.'

Hardy's horse was led away to join the others at their place of concealment in the brush. Hardy accepted a full plate and a steaming cup and went to work on his chuck. Weston questioned him further about the missing stock and quickly concluded that the old hand knew what he was talking about. It looked as if his hunch were going to pay off, he reflected exultantly.

He felt differently about it the following morning. After another night of weary waiting, the dawn broke as peacefully as the night had passed. Outsmarted again! The punchers swore in weary disgust and discussed the matter pro and con. Weston stood a little apart, gazing with unseeing eyes down the pass, a concentration furrow deep between his black brows.

'Maybe they went some other way,' hazarded Jeth Bass, who was comparatively new to the section and not as thoroughly familiar with its peculiarities as were the others.

'Ain't no other way,' grunted Hardy. 'This crack is the only way through the hills for anything 'cept a lizard or a mountain goat.'

Weston suddenly turned. 'Sam,' he said, 'I

believe Jeth is right; they did go another way.'

'Which way?' snorted Hardy.

'By way of the Tornaga Desert,' Weston replied.

Hardy stared at him as if fully convinced he held converse with a lunatic.

'Have you gone plumb loco?' he demanded. 'Drive a herd of cows across that near forty miles of waterless inferno, the last fifteen or so of it nothing but dust and rocks and blinding heat. They *might* be able to run 'em the first twenty, travelling at night and with a stopover at a canyon about a dozen miles to the south where there's a spring, but on to the Border across the real desert? Don't make me laugh; my jaws are sore!'

'Go ahead and laugh,' Weston replied. 'I'm playing a hunch that they did go that way. They didn't go through the pass, that's for certain, and as I said before, Haynes would never keep the herd holed up somewhere to the north, especially knowing as he does that we've been scouring the country up there. He must have kept them on the move. Well, there's one way to find out. We're leaving here, skirting the west end of the hills and heading south — that is, if we can pick up a trail, which I'm willing to bet you a few pesos we do.'

'Done!' said Hardy. 'I can use a few pesos. Let's go.'

'You know, it's just possible that there's water down there somewhere,' Weston remarked as they got under way. 'Say out in the desert a way. They could do it if there is.'

'Uh-huh, and if a bullfrog had wings he wouldn't have to bump his belly on the ground,' snorted old Sam. 'If there's water down there how come desert rats who've been wandering over that section for years ain't found it? Those old coots are always nosing around hoping to make a strike. Remember I was born and brought up in this section, and if there was such a thing, I'd surely have heard about it.'

'It's getting too darn hot to argue,' said Weston, 'but if there's an answer to the question, down there's the place to find it.'

'Okay,' answered Hardy. 'But if a bad storm kicks up while we're down there — well, that desert will make a first-class buryin' place. The sun will bake us dry and the drifting sands will cover us up, and when we get to purgatory we won't notice any difference.'

They rounded the west wall of the hills

and turned south, eyes eagerly scanning the earth.

'Spread out and we'll quarter the ground,' Weston directed. A little later he reined in and called to Hardy.

'Guess you'd better fork over those pesos, Sam,' he said.

Hardy swore incredulously, damning his eyes for revealing to him what didn't exist. But he was unable to refute the evidence that a herd of cattle *had* passed that way, headed south, with shod horses pacing them, not more than thirty hours before. Weston, riding back and forth across the well-defined trail of hoof marks, made another discovery.

'And it's not the first herd that's passed this way. There were others, quite a while back. The old prints show plain over here where the ground is softer.' Hardy shook his grey thatch and muttered under his breath.

'Not pushing them very fast,' Weston observed as they rode south again.

'Heading 'em for that canyon I told you about, where there's a mite of water,' Hardy grunted.

For nearly two hours they rode at a good pace, following the prints that ran close to the slope of the hills, where the heat was not so intense. Finally Hardy, who was thoroughly familiar with the section, suggested that they slow down.

'Mighty likely, I'd say, that the hellions are holed up in that canyon right ahead,' he explained. 'I figure they wouldn't go past that.'

Jim Weston smiled and said nothing. However, he heeded the old puncher's warning, and they approached the canyon mouth with caution. Nothing happened; no sound broke the silence. They reached a point hugging the hill wall, from which they could peer into the gorge. It was scantily brush-grown and there were no signs of occupancy, although the line of prints they were following turned into it. From the mouth flowed a trickle of water that quickly lost itself in the thirsty sands.

'Reckon they went on up that crack,' Hardy remarked uncertainly.

Weston gestured to the others to enter the canyon and let their horses drink from the small spring there. He himself rode on south until he had passed the gorge mouth, which was not very wide. He pulled up, scanned the ground ahead and rejoined his companions.

'Trail comes back out of the canyon and continues south,' he remarked to Hardy.

The only answer he got was a rumble of profanity.

After men and horses had enjoyed a hearty drink from the little spring, they resumed the trail. A little later they reached the southern terminus of the range of hills and were subjected to the full blast of the sun. Now the heat was withering.

'And you ain't seen nothing yet,' said Hardy. 'Wait till you hit the real desert. You'll think you're a beefsteak on a grid. I've been down there, and I know. Run cows across that with no water south of the spring back there!'

Weston merely pointed to the line of hoof marks dwindling away into the distance.

'Yeah, I see them,' sputtered Hardy, 'but they ain't there — can't be. Just one of them blasted mirages.'

'Jim, if you figure the hellions are headed for the Border, don't you figure they'll stop off at the canyon on their way back?' one of the hands observed. 'Might have been a good notion to wait for them there.'

'Not likely they'd stop there on the way back,' Weston replied. 'They'll be travelling fast and would keep on going, I'd say. Besides, I'm mighty curious to learn how they did it. We'll keep on south.'

Another hour and more passed. The sparse

vegetation disappeared altogether, and they were on the sands and alkali of the true desert. Here the heat struck like the breath of a blast furnace. As far as the eye could reach was a drab vista of arid sands and leprous alkali dust with nothing to relieve the dreary monotony except here and there a dead-looking cactus brandishing spiny and twisted arms like a devil in torment.

'Lucky there isn't any wind,' Weston remarked. 'It would fill the prints with sand in a hurry, and we'd have no trail to follow.'

The heat was increasing by the minute. Lips began to crack, tongues to swell. The horses snorted nervously and blew the dust from their nostrils.

Far to the south a dusky line of shadow materialised, dimly seen through the shimmer of the dancing heat devils. Soon it resolved into a narrow belt of chaparral.

'What's that?' Jeth Bass asked.

'That's the brush growing along the dry bed of what the old-timers called Lost River,' said Hardy. 'It ain't a river at all, just a dry wash. In the early spring, if the snow on the hills happens to melt fast, there's water in it, sometimes after real hard rains, too, but it don't last.'

'We had a real hard rain just a few days back,' Bass remarked hopefully.

'Doesn't mean anything,' Hardy replied. 'You don't measure the time the water stays in Lost River by days but by hours. Just a few hours after it stops raining it's all sunk in the sands and gone.'

'Seems a lot of brush growing there from just the spring snow water and an occasional rain,' Weston observed musingly.

'Well, there it is, no arguing that,' said Hardy. 'And there ain't no arguing the fact that the wind's starting to blow a mite,' he added significantly.

They reached the belt of chaparral, which was tinder dry and stood stiff and motionless under the scorching sun. As they forced their weary horses through the tangle, the upper leaves rustled under the hot breath of the wind.

The desert-wise Hardy shook his head dubiously. 'Jim,' he said, 'I'd advise staying right here for a spell till we see what that wind's going to do. It may not amount to much, but if a real storm kicks up, we could run into bad trouble out on the sand. This brush will shield us a bit from the dust and from the wind. And if it blows real hard, those prints are going to be filled up in a jiffy anyhow.'

'Expect you're right,' Weston acceded. 'We'll give the horses a breather and see what happens.'

They pushed forward to the sloping bank of the wide drywash, misnamed a river. Ten feet below was the bed — dry, packed sand, with a faint film of grey dust topping the sand. The surface was scored by innumerable hoof prints.

'Looks like they pranced around down there for an hour,' remarked Hardy.

'It sure does,' agreed Weston. 'And there's the trail leading up the far bank and heading on south. No doubt but they stopped here for a while. Sam, there *must* be water around here somewhere.'

Hardy was too tired and hot and thirsty to argue further. 'All right! All right!' he grumbled. 'Come on boys; comb the darn brush and show this young hellion he's mistaken.'

Weston remained on the river-bank, gazing at the multitude of prints below. They formed a definite pattern, not what might have been expected from the aimless churning of a milling herd. There were also the hoof marks of horses. Turning Ashes, he paced slowly down the bank. A hundred yards farther on the prints abruptly ceased. To all appearances the cattle had been turned there and sent back up the wash; also the horses. Reining Ashes about, he rode back the way he had come and continued for a short distance beyond his starting point. And again he reached a spot where the hoof marks abruptly discontinued. Weston swore in bewilderment.

Thoroughly puzzled, he dismounted and scrambled down the sloping bank. Squatting on his heels, he examined the prints. The edges were hard and caked, not at all what might have been expected in loose sand.

'Like they'd been made in mud,' he muttered, 'What in blazes?'

He stared about, seeking a solution to the mystery. Abruptly his gaze focused. Where the slope of the far bank joined the dusty bed was a faint, pale shimmer of green. Wonderingly, he made his way to it and paused in astonishment.

Just pushing through the earth were the tips of tiny plants. They were fresh and green!

Weston gazed at the unexplainable growth that could never have been born of dust and desiccation. Only life-giving moisture could account for such a phenomenon. He turned and studied the definite pattern of prints, the steady beat of hoofs up and down the dry bed, back and forth, back and forth. Bits of desert lore drifted across his mind, and fragments, half-forgotten, of geological facts retained from his schooldays. He studied the trough-like formation of the drywash and uttered a sharp exclamation:

'Blazes! I've got it!'

Chapter XVII

Weston scrambled up to the bank to where he had left Ashes. In answer to his shout, the cowboys came straggling back from their fruitless search of the brush.

'Fork your broncs,' he told them, 'down on to the bed of the wash, and ride back and forth, hard and steady.'

'Have you gone absolutely loco?' demanded Sam Hardy.

'Don't argue; do as I tell you,' Weston shot back at him. 'We'll have all the water we want in half an hour.'

Hardy let out a dismal wail. 'Better do as he says, boys,' he moaned. 'Humour him. Keep him from gettin' violent. Remember, he's chain-lightning on the draw, and he never misses. If all of a sudden he imagines we're prairie chickens or gophers, we're goners. Come on!'

Cursing and muttering, the bewildered punchers obeyed. Back and forth, back and forth, galloped the disgusted horses. Clouds of dust arose from under the pounding hoofs at first, but to the astonishment of everybody except Jim Weston, it ceased to rise as the sand packed tighter.

'Say!' an excited cowboy yelled. 'This stuff's getting soft and squishy!'

'My bronc's splashing!' another whooped.

'By Godfrey, there's water risin' through the sand!' roared Tom Peters. 'Well, if this don't take the shingles off the barn!'

Peters was right. There was an undoubted film of water covering the sands. Soon the thirsty horses were striving to thrust their muzzles into it. Weston watched the water rise to three or four inches in depth.

'All right; get the horses over to the bank,' he called. 'You'll have something like quicksand there before long, and I expect that under the caked sand crust is real quicksand. If a cayuse busts through that crust, he's liable to go out of sight in a minute, and the jigger who's forking him, too. Besides, we don't want that water to rise too high. Come out of it!'

The cowboys obeyed the warning, allowing their horses to drink only after they had reached firm ground. Then they absorbed as much of the liquid as they could hold. Sam Hardy squatted beside Weston and rolled a cigarette.

'Jim,' he asked, 'how in blazes did you figure it?'

'It was that mess of hoof marks down there on the river-bed that first set me to wondering,' Weston explained. 'Why the devil should anybody run a bunch of cows and horses, burning up with thirst and exhausted as they must have been, up and down a dry river-bed! I figured there must have been a reason. And I concluded that in some way that reason must have been connected with the water they so sorely needed. But I really began to catch on when I spotted that patch of green stuff over there under the bank. I knew those shoots could never have come up without moisture somewhere close by. While I was wracking my brains over that, I recalled hearing an old-timer telling my father about pounding water up through the sand of an Arizona desert. Not exactly the same conditions as here, I imagine, but similar. Then while I was puzzling over that and wondering just how it was done, I began to remember some of the things I had learned about geology when I was in school. All of a sudden I had it.

'You see, there is a stratum of hard rock that forms the real river-bed, what was the bed of a real river thousands, perhaps millions of years ago, the bed that during the ages filled with sand. I imagine the bed, which is a sort of rock trough, is quite a way down. The sand, you'll notice, is smooth, round grains, the sort which makes quicksand when water flows over it. The sand becomes almost fluid and is held in suspension. But as the water level sinks, the sand on top quickly dries and packs hard. The sand and water mixed beneath support the crust of dry sand, and the closely packed grains prevent the water beneath from evaporating.'

'Sort of a lake covered with sand,' Hardy interpolated.

'That's just about it,' acceded Weston. 'No wonder there's such a heavy stand of brush along the banks. Chances are snow water stays down there all summer, and every time it rains, more water trickles through the upper sand to replenish the supply. Some of the water, when it is high, seeps back in a couple of hours, and the river bed will be dry and dusty again. Incidentally, that's why I stopped the riding before the water rose very high. I want that bed to be dry by the time those hellions get back from the Border, which I imagine will be toward sundown.'

Old Sam shook his head in wordless admiration. Tom Peters chuckled.

'Reckon there's something to education, after all,' he observed. 'I never held much by book learnin', but I reckon it comes in handy at times. I sure won't argue the point after this. Now what do we do, Jim?'

'Hole up in the brush and wait,' Weston replied. 'It's about certain the bunch will come this way. They won't hang around the Border any longer than they have to. Always the chance of a patrol of *rurales* coming along, and they won't want to tangle with the Mexican mounted police. They'll stop here for water and to eat, the chances are, and then we'll hit them. Here's hoping Haynes is with them. I've a notion he will be. That was a big herd we've been trailing — a lot more than the two hundred Sam says we lost the other night. They may have been holding some in reserve somewhere. And I've a feeling Haynes would want to be along to supervise the disposal of that many head, and to collect payment.'

'Just let me line sights with him!' growled Peters. 'He's my meat.'

Choosing a spot from which they could see and not be seen, the Lucky Seven punchers made themselves as comfortable as conditions would permit. The wind had strengthened and howled overhead, but the thick growth kept off most of the flying dust and mitigated the heat somewhat. The water in the river had disappeared, and already the sand there was growing dusty under the beat of the sun.

A long and tedious wait followed. The punchers were nervous from strain and anticipation of the desperate battle that might well be confronting them. The sun sank in a lurid setting of blood and flame. It was almost full dark when Weston suddenly exclaimed:

'Get set! Here they come.'

The others also heard the click of irons nearing the far bank. A few more minutes, and from their place of concealment they saw shadowy figures ride down to the river-bed.

'They'll pound up some water, and then they'll light a fire and cook a meal,' Weston whispered. 'Wait till they get the fire going good and are ganged around it. We'll give them a chance to surrender, but I'm afraid they won't give up without a fight. If it starts, shoot straight and shoot fast; they won't show us any mercy if they get the upper hand.'

The thudding of hoofs on the dry sands continued for some time. The clean-cut sound gradually changed to a sucking and gurgling. Soon the owlhoot band came streaming up the near bank. Weston counted nine of the shadowy shapes.

Close to the north wall of brush, where it curved to the south-east and provided a wind-break, a fire was kindled. Preparations for a meal began. The outlaws grouped around the fire.

Tom Peters hissed exultingly, for looming above his companions was the tall form of Nelson Haynes.

'All right,' Weston whispered, 'let's go!' He stepped forward into the little clearing flanked by the brush, the others fanning away on either side. His voice rang out:

'Elevate! You're covered!'

The outlaws whirled at the sound. For an instant they stood paralysed with astonishment. Then Nelson Haynes, with a yell of fury, went for his gun. The growth rocked and shivered to the roar of six-shooters.

But this time conditions favoured the cowboys, who were but shadows against the dark growth, while the wide-loopers were clearly outlined by the glare of the fire. Half their number went down at that first flaming volley. The others scattered, blazing away at the cowhands. One, reeling and staggering, ran straight through the fire, kicking glowing embers in every direction. They showered upon the tinder-dry leaves and twigs beneath the growth. The fierce breath of the wind caught them, and even as the guns flashed and thundered, a roaring sheet of flame shot upward.

'Back!' yelled Weston. 'Back to the horses! Hightail!'

His followers obeyed, tearing through the brush with the flames roaring at their heels. The outlaws who remained alive also dived for their horses, but too late. The frenzied animals went crashing away through the burning growth, their panic-stricken masters racing blindly after them.

All but Nelson Haynes. Weston saw the tall leader dive over the river-bank and land with a splash in the shallow water. Instantly he leaped after the Bar H owner. Gun spurting fire, he plunged down the slope and into the water. Haynes was ploughing for the far bank and was already half-way across. A bullet from Weston's gun grazed his cheek and sent him reeling. He whirled to face his pursuer. Weston snapped a shot at him, knew he had missed. He slewed sideways as Haynes fired in return. The bullet knocked his left-hand gun spinning and numbed his arm to the shoulder. He took deliberate aim with his remaining Colt and pulled the trigger. The hammer clicked on an empty shell.

With a yell of triumph, Haynes threw down with his gun. But even as he lined sights, the yell changed to a scream of terror. Weston, frantically striving to reload, stared with bulging eyes. Haynes had suddenly decreased in stature. He was an absurdly short mannikin, his shoulders barely rising above the surface of the shallow water. His gun fell from his hand, and he thrashed madly with both arms. Jim Weston understood.

'Good God! He broke through the crust; the quicksand's got him!' he gasped aloud.

At the same instant he felt the river-bed heave and quiver beneath his feet, Alive to his own deadly danger, he plunged madly for the bank. Behind him sounded a bubbling shriek, chopped off as by the sweep of a great knife.

Gasping and panting, Haynes' despairing scream ringing in his ears, Weston fought toward the shore. The sands shifted and yielded beneath his floundering feet. They coiled about his legs like the tentacles of an octopus. One foot plunged down, and it took the last vestige of his strength to draw it up again. The sands gripped his knees, rising to his thighs as, with a final frenzied effort, he hurled himself forward and felt the crust break beneath his feet.

But with that last supreme effort of despair, his hands came down on solid ground. He clawed hard earth, clutched at boulders, got a hold on a projecting root. With a superhuman burst of strength he dragged himself forward a few inches. He gripped another tough mesquite root with bleeding fingers, heaved upward, shoved back with his other hand. Gurgling and sucking, clinging like a constricting snake, the sullen muck yielded, and he floundered on to the dry bank.

Instantly a new terror confronted him. It seemed he had escaped death by suffocation only to succumb to an even more agonising one by fire. On the crest of the bank the flames leaped and roared. Stinging embers showered his body and hissed in the water to which he dared not return. He hugged the bank, forced his body beneath a shallow overhang and lay coughing and choking, his wet clothes steaming from the heat. His head was whirling, his senses leaving him. And if unconsciousness loosened the cord of his fingers that dug into the earth and clung, he would slide down the steep slope to the quicksand and perish.

Numbly he realised that the heat was lessening. The fierce draught sucked in by the flames, aided and abetted by the wind blowing from the south-east, was driving the fire back from the lip of the bank. The embers no longer fell; the air was clearing. Overhead the murk thinned. A shaft of moonlight struggled through and silvered the sinking waters. One spot near the centre of the stream still swirled and eddied slightly. Weston turned from it with a shudder and cautiously climbed up the bank.

Beyond the smoking belt of growth voices were calling anxiously. He raised a reassuring shout in reply, but nearly an hour elapsed before he could cross the burned-over section and join his companions.

'Nobody bad hurt,' Sam Hardy replied to his question. 'Just some nicks and scratches. The wide-loopers? All shot or roasted 'cept one we grabbed when he came tumbling out of the brush blind from smoke. We got him over there by the horses. What happened to Haynes?'

Weston told him. 'I'll never forget the look on his face as he went down,' he concluded. 'It was an awful way to die.'

'The sidewinder had it coming,' rumbled Tom Peters. 'Reckon right now the devil's dryin' him out so he'll roast proper without sizzlin'. We caught their horses and the saddle-pouches of one — Haynes, I reckon

— is stuffed with money. Between three and four thousand dollars, I'd say.'

'Payment for the herd,' Weston nodded. 'Well, that'll help make up for what we've lost. I want to talk to the hellion you dropped a loop on.' He walked over and surveyed the dejected prisoner with cold eyes.

'Might be a good idea to answer a few questions, fellow,' he said. 'Otherwise we might take a notion to hold court right here. Still a few branches left standing, and we've got plenty of rope. Suppose you tell us what you know about Haynes.'

Taking the hint, the outlaw became voluble.

'I first met Haynes in a jail up in Kansas,' he said. 'There was about a dozen of us in there, waiting trial for cow stealing, when they brought him in with his head tied up. He'd killed a feller over a card game. He was smart and showed us how to bust out of jail. We stole horses and headed west. Haynes knew his business, and we did mighty well — couple of express cars, stages packing payrolls, small town banks. We circled through Nevada and California and into Arizona. Rustled some cows in the San Simon and Animas Valleys, but things were a mite hot thereabouts and we slid over into

New Mexico. Give me a cigarette, will you?'

Peters rolled him one, and he resumed his yarn.

'As I said, Haynes was smart. He said what we needed was a cover-up. So he bought a ranch and hired cowhands to work it. Us fellers kept out of sight, like we did here in a cabin he set up for us not too far from his ranch-house — I'll take you to it, if you want me to. Pickings weren't too good in New Mexico, so when he got a chance to sell, he decided we'd better move on. We came over here, and he figured this was about right. We took on some fellers from around here, but they all had bad luck.'

'And I've a notion the rest of you would have had "bad luck" after Haynes didn't have any more use for you,' Weston commented. 'Go on.'

'Uh-huh, he was smart, and eddicated,' the prisoner resumed. 'He was all the time roaming around looking things over. He found this infernal dry river and figured mighty quick water could be pounded up through the sand. We used the way across the desert when the sheriff and his deputies were snooping about in the hills around the pass. We were doing real well, but for some reason Haynes wanted that blasted Lucky Seven Ranch and began doing all sorts of loco things to get it. If it hadn't been for that we'd have done all right. You say he's dead? Blast him, anyhow! Guess that's about all I got to tell you that you don't already know.'

'It's enough,' said Weston, 'and it may make things a mite easier for you when you come to trial. Well, I guess we'd better head for home, boys. The horses are tired, but it will be cooler travelling at night, and we'll take the short cut straight north.'

The sun was well up when the sight of the Lucky Seven ranch-house gladdened the eyes of the exhausted horses and men. Leah came running to meet them as they pulled up in the yard.

'Good heavens! What happened?' she asked Weston. 'You look half-dead, and your shirt is all burned full of holes! Never mind. Come in, and I'll fix you coffee and something to eat. Then you can tell me.'

Weston told her as he ate. 'Yes, Haynes was a smart man,' he concluded. 'He had everything calculated to make him eminently successful. But there was a twist in his brain that turned him to a crooked trail. Somehow, though, I'm glad I didn't kill him. As it was, it looked as if Providence decided to take a hand and put an end to his evildoing.'

Leah repressed a shiver.

'And now,' Weston said, 'I'm going to bed and sleep a week.'

'No, you won't,' Leah replied. 'You may go to bed, but you're not going to sleep a week. Tomorrow you and I are going to ride to town.'

'What for?'

'Do you need to ask? To get married.'

ABOUT THE AUTHOR

Leslie Scott was born in Lewisburg, West Virginia. During the Great War, he joined the French Foreign Legion and spent four years in the trenches. In the 1920s he worked as a mining engineer and bridge builder in the western American states and in China before settling in New York. A barroom discussion in 1934 with Leo Margulies, who was managing editor for Standard Magazines, prompted Scott to try writing fiction. He went on to create two of the most notable series characters in Western pulp magazines. In 1936, Standard Magazines launched, and in *Texas Rangers,* Scott under the house name of **Jackson Cole** created Jim Hatfield, Texas Ranger, a character whose popularity was so great with readers that this magazine featuring his adventures lasted until 1958. When others eventually began contributing Jim Hatfield stories, Scott created another Texas Ranger hero,

Walt Slade, better known as *El Halcon,* the Hawk, whose exploits were regularly featured in *Thrilling Western.* In the 1950s Scott moved quickly into writing book-length adventures about both Jim Hatfield and Walt Slade in long series of original paperback Westerns. At the same time, however, Scott was also doing some of his best work in hardcover Westerns published by Arcadia House; thoughtful, well-constructed stories, with engaging characters and authentic settings and situations. Among the best of these, surely, are *Silver City* (1953), *Longhorn Empire* (1954), *The Trail Builders* (1956), and *Blood on the Rio Grande* (1959). In these hardcover Westerns, many of which have never been reprinted, Scott proved himself highly capable of writing traditional Western stories with characters who have sufficient depth to change in the course of the narrative and with a degree of authenticity and historical accuracy absent from many of his series stories.

We hope you have enjoyed this Large Print book. Other Thorndike, Wheeler, Kennebec, and Chivers Press Large Print books are available at your library or directly from the publishers.

For information about current and upcoming titles, please call or write, without obligation, to:

Publisher
Thorndike Press
10 Water St., Suite 310
Waterville, ME 04901
Tel. (800) 223-1244

or visit our Web site at:

http://gale.cengage.com/thorndike

OR

Chivers Large Print
published by AudioGO Ltd
St James House, The Square
Lower Bristol Road
Bath BA2 3SB
England
Tel. +44(0) 800 136919
email: info@audiogo.co.uk
www.audiogo.co.uk

All our Large Print titles are designed for easy reading, and all our books are made to last.